Magic, Mystery, Madness

Magic, Mystery, Madness

Electric Ekphrastics

Andrew Geyer
Terry Dalrymple
Jerry Craven

Edited by Tom Mack

ISBN: 978-0-9987364-6-4
Library of Congress Control Number: 2022943516
Manufactured in the United States
graphic images by Jerry Craven

Angelina River Press
Fort Worth, Texas

Acknowledgments

We are grateful to the editors of the 2020 issue of *Windward Review* for publishing a preview of this book, which included two stories: "Clarissa's Spirit" (published here as "Green-Eyed Spirit") by Terry Dalrymple and "The Nightwatch" by Andrew Geyer; two poems by Jerry Craven, "This Strange Malachite Art" and "Rosita's Instructions to the Painter," as well as the four graphics that go with the writing. The issue of *Windward Review* is available in print as well as online.

Thanks to the editorial staffs of the following journals for publishing some of the fiction now in *Magic, Mystery, Madness*:

Writing Texas: Terry Dalrymple's "How Millard Mack Became Crippled: A Love Story"

Concho River Review: Jerry Craven's "Uncle Marvin Smoked a Worm"

Viva Texas Rivers: Andrew Geyer's "Things Water Whispers to Limestone"

Cimarron Review: Andrew Geyer's "So Many Lovely Lies"

We appreciate the East Texas Art League for hosting Jerry Craven's art show "Magical Realism," an exhibit that prompted Craven, Dalrymple, and Geyer to begin this book. Also thanks to the art league for awarding a blue ribbon to the graphic art "A Walk Beyond the Moon" in their 2021 fall/winter art show.

Promise me, baby, that you'll be my
footprint on the moon
Andrew Geyer

CONTENTS

Full Page Graphic art

The cardinal opened its wings and flew farther up into the sky than it had ever been, then swooped low over the lake in a blur of red.

Terry Dalrymple

Introduction

Tom Mack

What's in a word? Derived from the Greek, the term "ekphrasis" is actually an eighteenth-century coinage. Some unknown classicist plundered his store of academic Greek to come up with a term he could use to label the extended description of objects often found in ancient texts like Homer's *Iliad*. The prefix "ex" or "out" paired with the verb "phrasein" or "to speak" seemed to do the trick.

Although the exact origin of the term is unknown, what is clear is that this word, which was originally coined to refer to any passage of detailed verbal description, eventually became more specialized in meaning. By the next century, ekphrasis was used to refer almost exclusively to a work of poetry that sought to represent or reflect upon the scene depicted in a painting or sculpture. Take, for example, the antics of the "marble men and maidens" in John Keats's "Ode on a Grecian Urn" or the fall of Icarus as depicted in Pieter Bruegel the Elder's famous sixteenth-century landscape painting and subsequently translated into verse by W.H. Auden in "Musee des Beaux Arts."

Over time, the definition of the ekphrastic act has expanded its range of relevant genres to encompass prose writing, particularly short fiction; and this brings us to the present day and the extraordinary accomplishment of three innovative Texans, whose verbal interactions with visual art embrace both poetry and prose.

The success of an ekphrastic response depends, it can be argued, on the choice of a compelling subject. In this volume, we encounter the luminous and inspiring works that Jerry Craven has produced by using his computer screen as his canvas and assorted software programs as his virtual paintbrush. Printed versions of Craven's digital wizardry first saw the light of day in an exhibit organized by the East Texas Art League in 2020. These works of pictorial art were, to a considerable extent, the result of years of Jerry Craven's experimentation as both a graphic designer—in his role as the publisher of Lamar University Literary Press he was often called upon to design book covers—and an avid photographer.

The nearly eighty images assembled in this volume for the first time combine often vintage photographic elements with the extraordinary views of our neighboring planets as well as distant stars and galaxies, captured by the Hubble Space Telescope. In essence, they combine the terrestrial with the celestial. Consider, for example, the cover image with its bearded gentleman in formal dress, who has presumably parked his classic automobile somewhere in the desert Southwest in order to consult a giant astrolabe. The functions of this ancient astronomical instrument include the practical, such as calculating latitude and generating tide tables, and the mystical, such as determining Muslim prayer times. While the gentleman on the cover stares intently at his scientific tool, the night sky above him shimmers with light, and planets float in improbable altitudes.

In each compelling image in this collection, Jerry Craven gives the viewer something easily relatable—a young woman out for a stroll or the illuminated waterfront of a picturesque town—but he imbeds these elements in a context that defies time and space and rational probability. The young woman in "A Walk Beyond the Moon" follows a trail that seems to wind its way through a nebula of blue and red space dust; the harbor front in "Our Vast and Present Moment" is framed by a starry sky above and below. With his playful juxtaposition of component parts and his ramped-up color palette, Craven enhances the visual magic of each piece.

Jerry Craven himself has described his visual approach as "graphic magic realism," borrowing a term from the literary realm used to describe a work grounded in the real world but imbued with an undercurrent of fantasy or, in this case, "magic, mystery, madness." Indeed, in this innovative volume, we find a blend of the natural and supernatural both in the visual works that are the reference point of each ekphrastic tale or poem and also in those verbal texts that both respond to and pivot around those pictorial images.

In responding to Craven's visual stimuli, all three literary artists—Andrew Geyer, Terry Dalrymple, and Craven himself—agreed on at least one basic ground rule when they embarked on their year-and-a-half collaborative project: in their responsive poem or story, they pledged to make reference to items found in the graphic work. Thus, in Terry Dalrymple's tale "Egret Angel," a white heron such as the one pictured in Craven's graphic art knocks on the narrator's front door; in Andrew Geyer's story "The Magical Bunnell Place," the marsh-surrounded bungalow in Craven's image supplies the story's primary setting.

It is obvious, as well, that the most effective verbal responses to Jerry Craven's visual stimuli not only incorporate both the celestial and terrestrial elements of the visual reference work but also transcend the merely representational to take the reader to places only hinted at within the picture frame. In Jerry Craven's tale "Seeds of Power," for example, the narrator visits a far-distant planet to confront a character not unlike Kurtz in Joseph Conrad's "Heart of Darkness." Terry Dalrymple's short story "The Woman Who Never Smiled" provides multiple explanations why the star-gazing female in Jerry Craven's enigmatic image is so crestfallen. Andrew Geyer's narrative response to Craven's visual construct entitled "How You Say Home" reveals how the place of one's birth is both a burden and a blessing. In addition to the joy to be found in the interplay of two art forms—the visual and the literary—subsumed in the ekphrastic act, this groundbreaking volume is structured in such a way to make the reading experience even more engaging.

The contents are organized into eleven three-part fascicles, each bundle focusing on a single concept or unifying image and each highlighting one piece by each member of the talented threesome. The book is also effectively capped off with a novella penned by Dalrymple, Geyer, and Craven in response to multiple graphic referents. There is so much to engage the eye and mind in this single volume! What's in a word? The term coined by an anonymous eighteenth-century scholar trying to label a rhetorical device popular in ancient texts has morphed over time in the hands of poets and fiction writers alike. In this volume, subtitled "electric ekphrastics," we confront, however, something fairly far removed from the lyrical world of John Keats. This is a place, both visual and verbal, where both Jules Verne and Isaac Asimov might feel at home, a place informed by the evolution of modern science fiction and the technological advances that have made possible Jerry Craven's stunning computer-manipulated images. Electric ekphrastics, indeed!

1. Moonglow

A Walk Beyond the Moon

A Walk Beyond the Moon

Andrew Geyer

1. Captivated

Six-year-old Lucy Storey first heard that word in the late afternoon of July 20, 1969, and it perfectly described the way she felt that evening about Peepaw's doll. About what she'd seen of it, that is. What she'd managed to see. She was sure she'd feel the same way about the rest, but even more so, when she finally held the doll in her arms. While her grandfather sat staring at the mock-up of the lunar lander squatting like a bug on the simulated surface of the moon on TV, Lucy sneaked glimpse after glimpse of the partially hidden figure on his lap—catching flickers of fiery red hair and creamy skin that shone even brighter than the real moon floating in the South Carolina sky outside the living room window.

"Captivated." It was Peepaw's answer, earlier, when Lucy asked how he felt about her new sundress. The dress was deep blue, with a white Peter Pan collar and tiny white flowers that swirled in spirals from her shoulders to her knees. She'd worn it to church that morning, and put it back on right before her daddy dropped her off at her grandfather's house to watch the first-ever time a man would walk on another world—and the mix of wonder and love on her Peepaw's sun-leathered face had made the meaning of the word perfectly clear without her needing to ask.

And now, after three giant bowls of Jiffy Pop and more than two hours sitting on the living room rug next to Peepaw's big green La-Z-Boy recliner, Lucy sneaked her longest glimpse yet—and felt so captivated she could barely breathe. He thought he had it hidden in the folds of the orange-and-yellow afghan that Meemaw crocheted before she passed. But through the gaps in the loose-knit weave, Lucy plainly made out a dainty white hat, red cork-screw curls, milky white skin, and blue eyes that fairly gleamed with life. She'd never even heard of a doll like this, much less seen one, and she had dozens (Peepaw was always "surprising" her with dolls). There was Barbie and her English friend Stacey (Lucy had met real English people at the stable Peepaw took her to for riding lessons), Barbie's younger sister Skipper and baby sister Tutti, and of course Barbie's boyfriend Ken. Peepaw even gave Lucy a Christie doll once. But her daddy wouldn't let her keep it because Christie was black (*black* wasn't the word Daddy used when he snatched the doll away, but Lucy didn't like to think about that word or the ugly way her daddy sounded when he said it).

"Peepaw? How long till the astronauts start their moonwalk?" she asked at last.

"We've still got a while, baby. First the folks in Mission Control have to decide that it's safe for them to come out of the lander."

"I wish I had something to do while we're waiting," she said in her sweetest I-love-you-Peepaw voice. "I didn't bring along anything to play with."

"Why don't you play a little something on the piano instead?"

"Don't you have anything else for me to do?"

"Well, I might have a little something for later. To celebrate Neil Armstrong stepping onto the lunar surface. Right now, won't you please play that Schumann piece we've been working on? Play 'Lonely Flowers.'"

2. *Lonely*

Robert J. Storey learned the true meaning of that word on September 23, 1918, when his beloved Millie died of the Spanish flu. She was nineteen years old, pregnant with what they were both sure would be a beautiful baby girl. The gaping hole that double loss—the love of his life, and the tiny unborn life they'd sparked together—ripped in the fabric of Robert's existence had never mended.

Music, especially writing and playing music on the piano, was the main thing that had kept him on planet Earth for the past fifty years. His current piano, a Baldwin Acrosonic upright, sat in the center of one living room wall surrounded by built-in shelves filled with books. If not for the piano, the books, his enduring hope for a little girl to dote on, and his flower garden out back, Robert would long ago have joined Millie and their unborn baby daughter in the infinite space beyond the moon.

"Lonely flowers," he said, catching Lucy's eye and pointing up at the bouquet of freshcut white rainflowers atop the piano. "See? It's not just me who wants to hear you play the Schumann piece. The flowers are lonesome for a bit of music."

"But how can the flowers be lonesome when they're all bunched together?"

"Some of the loneliest times in my life have come in middle of a bunch of people." He was thinking now of his second wife, Ethel, and their four sons. But he was too much of a gentleman to say so. "I never feel even a little bit lonely, though, when I'm with you."

"What about when you're not with me, Peepaw?"

"Every minute." He pulled the sheet music from the piano bench, and two of them sat down."Now, do you remember what I told you about the opening of 'Lonely Flowers?'"

"Slow and easy?"

"Good girl," he said, glancing at the corner TV where Walter Cronkite and Wally Schirra were still talking about the upcoming moonwalk. He didn't want Lucy to miss the big moment. She eased into the piece just the way he'd taught her. As she worked her way through, occasionally hitting a wrong note, he glanced back and forth between her delicate fingers on the ivory keys and the TV that was now showing row upon row of black-tied men in Mission Control. In his mind the white-shirted men in their black ties and the black and white piano keys swirled together so that he and his granddaughter became a part of something much larger than themselves. He'd bought the new color TV, a state-of-the-art RCA Home Entertainment Center, specifically for the moonshot. It had set him back a pretty penny, but it was worth it to make sure his only granddaughter saw history being made. Here in this house. With him.

And that she felt like she was part of it. All the rest of his descendants were boys, four sons and seven grandsons. Lucy was the youngest of the grandchildren, blonde and blue-eyed and heartbreakingly beautiful. But the decade that was ending, the only decade she'd ever known, had been so filled with madness—violence at home and abroad—the Cold War, the Vietnam War, the Kennedys dead, Martin Luther King dead, so many dead. He wanted Lucy to understand that the moonwalk they were about to witness was important. He wanted her to see that there was hope.

As the final chord of "Lonely Flowers" faded, tears blurred Robert's vision and he blinked hard to keep them back. "That was lovely," he said at last. "The best I've heard you play it yet."

"Why don't you play something, Peepaw? I know! Play 'Clair de Lune.' It's your very best thing. Maybe it'll get Neil Armstrong to finally come out of the lander."

"All right, baby. Slow and easy," he said, and started in.

3. *Simulation*

The word stretched across the bottom of the TV screen as the hatch of the mock-up lunar lander opened and a man in a bulky white space suit appeared. Another man in a space suit held a rope that he slowly let out as the first man descended. Then suddenly the picture changed, and the man with the rope tied to him was standing outside the lander. He was supposed to be on a ladder, but it looked to Lucy like he was standing on a big gold-colored box as her Peepaw came to the end of "Clair de Lune."

"Sim-u-lation," she said hesitantly, feeling out the syllables and trying to sound like the announcers—who kept saying the word over and over—as the picture changed again. "What does it mean, Peepaw?"

"It means *pretend*. That man on the ladder there is pretending to be Neil Armstrong. They're simulating the beginning of the moon-walk. But we should get the real thing momentarily."

"I told you if you played 'Clair de Lune' you'd get them to come out. Didn't I tell you, Peepaw?" He was the smartest man she knew—maybe the smartest in the world—and just about every wall in his house was covered with shelves full of books. Then the TV picture changed again. It was blurry and a little bit confusing because it looked like the man on the ladder was upside-down. And the word *simulation* had been replaced by the words *live from the surface of the moon.*

"There it is!" her grandfather shouted, and they rushed back over to their places in front of the TV. "That's the real Neil Armstrong, the mission commander."

The picture flipped again, so the man on the ladder was rightside-up. The bulky man with his big backpack climbed slowly down. He paused, and several voices talked back and forth on the TV about what he was doing and why. Then he stepped with both feet off the ladder and landed on the lunar surface that gleamed silvery white.

"That's one small step for man," he said, "one giant leap for mankind."

The TV announcers didn't seem to have understood the words; but Lucy heard them clearly, although she wasn't quite sure what they meant. She realized vaguely that she hadn't breathed for a while, almost like she'd been underwater—kind of like Neil Armstrong looked as he bobbed up and down on the surface of the moon.

Then the picture changed again. Everything went white. Neil Armstrong was white and the surface of the moon was white.

"Like a ghost," her grandfather said, "walking on the specter of a moon."

And Lucy didn't know what to think about that.

4. *Footprint*

The concept underlying that word was the reason Robert J. Storey and his granddaughter were sitting together in front of a brand-new TV. While the astronauts were breaking out a motion picture camera, Walter Cronkite was talking about the first words spoken on the surface of the moon, about the bottom step of the ladder being damaged but usable, about moon dust being powdery and a bit sticky but walkable. Then he talked about the mark Neil

Armstrong had made on the moon.

"Footprint," Cronkite said, in summary of Armstrong's historical first step. "He can see his footprint in the fine particles."

"Lucy," Robert said, looking from the ghostly astronaut in black-and-white to her technicolor-lovely face, "this really is a giant leap for mankind. And womankind, too. Don't ever let your daddy or any of your uncles or brothers tell you any different. You're smarter than all of them put together. You're going to fly faster and farther, I can promise you that. And you're going to make a footprint of your own." The look on his granddaughter's face was confused, almost afraid, and Robert realized that his tone had been harsher than he intended.

"I'm sorry, baby," he said softly. "I didn't mean to growl. But it's crucial you understand that, for you, anything is possible. Will you promise to remember that?"

"I promise, Peepaw."

"Good girl." He pulled out the antique doll he'd been hiding underneath the afghan. "I want you to have this. But before I let you keep it forever, you'll have to make me another promise."

5. *Iris*

It was the name of the doll her Peepaw had just placed into Lucy's arms. But she was so excited to be finally holding the fiery-haired, blue-eyed fairy creature that she barely registered her grandfather's words.

"Iris," he said again. "Her name is Iris. But *iris* is also a kind of flower. And the iris flower is exactly the same color as your new baby's eyes."

"But she isn't really a baby, Peepaw. She looks more like a little girl. And why is her skin so shiny?"

"Iris is a China doll. An antique, and very fragile. I keep her in a special box in the attic, and I only bring her down once a year. Every September 23rd, in the evening, Iris and I go out for a walk."

"Where do you walk to?"

"To Bethany Cemetery at the end of the street. And it isn't just Iris and me. We take along a bouquet of white rainflowers for company, and a single blue iris flower."

"I don't understand."

"Before I married your Meemaw, I was married to someone else. Her name was Millie, and she was as lovely as any star in the firmament, and every bit as fiery. Would you like to see?"

"Okay."

Peepaw disappeared into his office and came back carrying a wooden trunk that he set down next to the TV. "This is Iris's special box," he said, swinging open the lid and rummaging around inside. "But I also keep some other things in it. Things that remind me of Millie." Sitting on the floor with Iris on her lap, Lucy carefully took the black-and-white photo that her Peepaw handed down to her. In the picture she saw a man in a black suit with a funny tie who looked very much like her Peepaw, but young. Beside him, in a white wedding dress, stood the most beautiful woman Lucy had ever seen. "She looks like Iris!" Lucy burst out, glancing back and forth between the picture and the doll.

"She does indeed. Although you can't tell it in the photo, Millie's eyes were exactly that same shade of blue." But it seemed to Lucy that her Peepaw's eyes had gone as faraway as the moon. "Millie was an orphan," he said slowly. "She grew up in the Charleston Orphan House and came up to Aiken County to work in the textile mills. We fell in love doing the foxtrot at

Hickman Hall in Graniteville and were married here in Aiken at St. Thaddeus Episcopal Church. It wasn't long before Millie was expecting. We were sure the baby would be a girl. So I took the trolley to Augusta and bought a gorgeous doll, in anticipation of the birth of our daughter. This doll. Iris." He reached out and gently brushed his fingers through the doll's hair. "But Millie died of the Spanish flu on September 23rd, 1918. The day before our first anniversary."

"But . . ." Lucy hesitated, seeing tears running down her grandfather's cheeks. "What happened to the baby, Peepaw?" Instead of answering, he walked over to the window and stared out at the moon. Lucy glanced away to the TV in the corner where the men on that same moon were using the motion picture camera they unloaded to make movies of themselves picking up rocks and putting them into a bag. Then the picture went blurry again, and Lucy said so.

"I know a place where we can get a better view," her grandfather said.

6. *Immortality*

Robert J. Storey wasn't sure about the possibility of such a thing. Much less the existence of a "heaven" where peace-parted souls spent eternity surrounded by family and friends. If it did exist, who would he see when he crossed over? Millie? Ethel? Would he get to choose?

"Maybe immortality," he whispered, "after all, is just a walk beyond the moon."

He took a flashlight from a drawer in the kitchen and the bouquet of rainflowers from the piano in the living room and led Lucy out into the front yard and down the sidewalk that ran along Newberry Street. Bethany Cemetery was just two blocks away, across Hampton Street, and they entered through a side gate that Robert knew to be chained but not locked. Tombstones and obelisks rose white in the moonlight ahead of them, climbing a low hill. There were only a few trees among the graves. The sky was incredibly visible. The stars hung low and thick, and the moon—a waxing crescent—looked like the fiery eye of a cosmic feline. As they walked out from under the trees that ringed the cemetery and in among the buried dead, Robert pointed at the moon above their heads.

"The men we just saw on TV," he said, "are standing on that bright white slice."

"I'll bet Neil Armstrong is looking down at the earth," Lucy said, "the same way we're looking up at him."

Robert led the way to a massive live oak whose branches cast dark shadows across the stars. Then he turned on the flashlight, revealing a headstone in the deep shade of the tree— an angel set upon a pedestal, both three feet tall, so that the eyes of the angel were on a level with Robert's eyes. The beam of light accentuated the angel's delicate grey features, her gossamer grey wings, her flowing gown of grey.

"This is Millie's grave, baby," Robert said. "You're not afraid, are you?"

"Not as long as I'm with you, Peepaw."

The cemetery was empty except for the two of them, completely quiet except for the crickets singing up at the summer moon. Robert stood next to Lucy at the foot of the grave. And even though Millie—what was left of Millie, her earthly remains—lay six feet below them, she still exerted a force akin to gravity. He felt himself drawn toward her like the tides to the moon. It was the same way he always felt when he stood in that place. There was a grey stone bench about six feet from the headstone. Robert sat down, and Lucy sat beside him.

"But I won't always be here with you," he said. "That's the reason we're sitting on this bench right now. It's the reason I gave you the doll."

"Iris."

"Yes. These rainflowers I'm carrying, they symbolize rebirth. Every year, on the anniversary of Millie's passing, I bring the doll to the cemetery. I also carry a bouquet of white rainflowers and a single blue iris. The iris, you see, symbolizes hope. I place the doll, along with the flowers, on this grave. Then I sit here on this bench, and I keep Millie and our unborn baby girl company. And I remember."

"But why no blue iris this time?"

"Because it's not September 23rd," Robert said. "When I married your Meemaw, she made me promise to move on. To focus on our future together. To never tell our children that I'd been married before. She even asked me to replace Millie's original tombstone, which I had made with both our names on it, for one with Millie's name alone." He took a deep breath, held it, let it out again. "I kept my word. Your Meemaw and I made a good life together, a life we shared with our sons and grandsons. And with you. It wasn't always a happy life. But it was good one. Which brings me to the promise I'd like to ask."

"What promise, Peepaw?"

"That you'll sit here with me every September 23rd, while I'm still in the land of the living. And that, after I'm gone, you'll remember me." He turned off the flashlight and silvery white light filtered down through the leaves. "Promise me, baby, that you'll be my footprint on the moon."

I know a plan can help shape the night.

Jerry Craven

Blue Moon

Blue Moon

Jerry Craven

The rare blue moon burst upon Annus
Horribilis 2020 in conjoining
with a blood moon flaming on All Hallow's Eve,
burning lunar bones and parched dirt:
two full moons calendar-pinned into one.
So we, cursed and covid ill in visionless
twenty-twenty hope for a good man
in the moon—but who has ever seen him?

Staged in a dream of midsummer night,
some saw the moon man actor-rogue
with ragged clothes, a lantern, a dog, a staff.
Medieval Germans claimed their full moon
carried a dirty-handed thief (lantern
dangling), stealing leeks and carrots, his dog
wearing speckled mange, its teeth bare
in snarling defense of moon man thievery.

We want the vision today to feel better,
a moon man top-hatted, leather
tailored, white gloves belying the German
digger of roots, a man holding his cane
with Victorian elegance, standing by a purebred dog,
his lantern made into art with leaded glass.

We know today the miracle of our old, dry
moon holding water, so now in a year
when we need miracles, might we dare
see a blue moonwater river rushing,
pushing back the fevered, diseased light?

When might we see the evasive elegance
of a good moon man, see a better vision
than 2020 might allow, delight
with a river alive and icy enough to hold
at bay the burning diseases of a terrible year?
Can there be hope while knowing visions are always
seldom, more rare than once in a blue moon?

Our Vast and Present Moment

Our Vast and Present Moment

Terry Dalrymple

Mary Louise Shaw, home from her second job, saw the scene she had come to expect. Her husband sat in his easy chair, beer in hand, fat cigar protruding from his mouth. The apartment reeked from the smoke. Five crushed beer cans had been tossed onto the coffee table, along with Chinese take-out cartons, one of which had tipped over and oozed brown liquid onto the table. When she passed his chair, he slanted his eyes toward her. She responded with a brief nod and kept walking. She didn't bother stepping into the kitchen, knowing all too well that he wouldn't think of getting take-out for her. But it didn't matter. She knew the routine and had eaten a sandwich at the bistro where she waited tables after a day of clerking at the department store.

In her room—they had months ago begun sleeping in separate rooms—she unzipped her dress, let it fall, and stepped out of the puddle of material. She flopped into her chair by the window. She was bone tired. From working two jobs for a total of sixteen hours, yes, but also from her dreary life. Just once, she thought, I'd like to feel happy again, alive again, and I'd like to see beauty again.

When they first married, she felt happy and alive always. He had ambitions and the energy, he claimed, to fulfill them. She wanted a house by the lake and eagerly anticipated the day they could afford one. But even now they still lived in a one-bedroom apartment a mile or more from the lake. His first business venture had failed utterly, and slowly that failure sucked up his ambition and energy. He worked part-time at the box factory, where he stood at a conveyor belt and watched for damaged or misshapen products, which he would remove and toss into a large bin behind him. He swore he was trying but simply couldn't get on full time or find another, better job. He had simply given up.

She stood and stepped to the window. At least their third-floor apartment provided a distant view of the calm lake water. She stared at it and the lights reflected on its surface. She longed to live right on its shore. She heard dogs, or maybe coyotes, yapping and howling some-where near the lake. Damned animals, she thought, disturbing the quiet evening in the pursuit of prey or in fear of danger. She sighed and fell back into the chair. Then, she changed her mind, stood, slipped her panties off, unhooked her bra, and dropped it on top of the panties. Nudity was the closest she could come to feeling free and unencumbered. She sat and sucked in a deep breath.

* * *

On the other side of town in a large, two-story house overlooking the lake, Robert "Shake" Perkins sipped slowly on his scotch, neat, the single drink he allowed himself each evening. It would help him sleep later. The evening news, volume turned low, lit his television screen, but he paid little attention, instead appreciating the large, framed photo of his wife. He had the photo enlarged and framed after her funeral. That had been almost a year before, and he still missed her desperately. He liked gazing at the photo and remembering their years together.

He knew that sadness was nothing new and certainly nothing unique. He had practiced family law for the past forty-two years and was no stranger to the many forms of jealousy, anger, sadness, disappointment, and loneliness of which the human heart is capable. And he was no exception, especially after his wife died. He had come to dislike his job but kept working because it was all he had to distract him, to fill his time. He longed for her laughter, her optimism, her ability to find beauty in virtually everything. He sipped his last bit of scotch, used the remote to darken the television. He arose and trudged upstairs to their bedroom. No, just his bedroom now. Unbuttoning his shirt, he looked out the window at the lake, a view she had always thrilled to. Moonlight and starlight shimmered on its surface, but he felt no thrill.

* * *

Downtown, a teenage boy, Billy Makins, ran a maze of dark alleys and side streets trying to evade the police officers who had come to get him. His breath weakened the longer he ran, and eventually he slowed to a trot, then to a vigorous walk. Stupid, he thought. Why was I so stupid? He had tried to buy the bottle of bourbon, sure that he wouldn't be carded. But the clerk turned out to be diligent. When the man asked for his ID, the boy just looked down and said nothing.

"Okay, kid," the clerk said. "Move along."

But the kid—he—had been stupid. He had grabbed the bottle and sprinted for the door. He glanced back to see the clerk already on the phone.

Finally, he stopped and bent, hands on knees, to catch his breath. Even if the police didn't find him, the clerk had gotten a good look. The cops would come, and his parents would let him sit in jail for a couple days before bailing him out. Damn. Why didn't he just walk away? Why did he grab that bottle? He had no answer. At the mouth of an alley, he threw the bottle into a dumpster and headed home, dreading his arrival. When he stepped into the

street, the light surprised him. It was an unlit street, but the moon and stars shone brighter than a street lamp. He looked up and admired them.

* * *

On the far side of the lake, a cardinal, out unusually late, perched on a short rock wall along a walking path. Its head bobbed up toward the sky, then down toward the lake, then side to side.

* * *

Mary Louise Shaw, in the drowse of almost-sleep, pushed herself up out of her chair. But before stumbling to bed, she once again stepped to the window. A full white moon hung high above the lake, its reflection brilliant. Far beyond the moonlight, bright stars dotted the darkness. She heard the dogs or coyotes. They weren't hunting, she thought, or confronting danger. They were barking at the moon, celebrating this moment when it shone so bright. The brightness of stars and moon mesmerized her, and she knew that beyond her sight more stars shone, other moons orbited other planets, all of them moving, circling, swirling, as they did day after day, night after night. They knew nothing of sadness or pain, they never paused, they simply swirled through a forever present moment. She felt awestruck by them, by this moment. And suddenly she wanted to share the moment with her husband. This moment, all moments. Not the past, not the future, just this moment and every moment of their lives. It was vast and it was now, now and always. It was a vast and present moment. Everyone's vast and present moment, she thought. Our vast and present moment. She felt calm, peaceful, blessed by the whole unfathomable universe. She murmured a prayer that everyone everywhere would know that moment, would feel that peace.

* * *

At that same moment, Robert "Shake" Preston, in his pajamas, pulling back the bed covers, felt an urge to return to the window. He fixed his eyes on the lake and the beautiful way it reflected the night sky, and he felt that his wife was looking with him, smiling, thrilled by the view. Of course she was with him, he realized, always with him, reveling in the exact moment of her place and time. He knew he would sleep well.

* * *

Admiring the night sky, Billy Makins didn't move. Soon, he would. He would go home, tell his parents what he did, spend a couple days locked up if he had to. But he would never miss another chance to enjoy moments like this. And he understood that moments like this were all moments if he just relaxed and stopped being stupid.

* * *

The cardinal opened its wings and flew farther up into the sky than it had ever been, then swooped low over the lake in a blur of red.

2. Transformation

The Nightwatch

The Nightwatch

Andrew Geyer

The sun has set at last on the summer solstice, Robert, and I begin my watch. Next to you here on the piano bench, I can almost feel your warmth as you start into "Clair de Lune." Almost. I ache for your touch, for the feel of your skin against my skin, for the weight of your body on mine. But like the plaintive chords of the third movement of Debussy's most famous piano suite, I am ethereal.

On this shortest night of the year, a full moon rides high in the South Carolina sky outside the living room window. In the light of that moon, which is the only light in the house, you look almost as ghostly as me. Almost.

According to pagan folklore, evil spirits appeared on the night of the summer solstice and magic of all kinds was at its strongest. As it turns out, those early pagans were right. Almost. It isn't just evil spirits, though, and we don't really appear—we're here all the time—but on the night of the summer solstice the barrier between the worlds is so thin we can be seen. Even touched.

But we can only make contact with those who are reaching out.

Instead of reaching out, Robert, you are looking inward. Looking back. Staring into the past the way you always do when you play those sad piano pieces. Debussy. Chopin. Satie. You sit alone in the dark, your hands stroking the keys instead of me, reliving that awful night five decades ago when I died in your arms.

"Stay with me, Millie," you said, your voice breaking. It was September 23rd, 1918. We were upstairs in our bedroom, and I lay dying of the Spanish flu. "Promise me. You have to stay, because I love you."

I was drowning, my lungs so full of fluid I could barely breathe. I wanted so badly to live for you, and for our unborn baby girl, more than I'd wanted anything ever before. "I . . . I promise," I managed, finally. Drowning, burning alive with fever, both at the same time.

Until suddenly, I wasn't.

Instead, I found myself standing next to you. You sat on the edge of our bed, staring down at the shell of flesh I'd just stepped out of. My skin was blue-tinged as a bruise, bloody froth rimmed my lips, and the China doll you'd bought for our daughter-to-be was propped up beside me on the pillows. You looked so young. So young, and so terribly sad. We both did. I'm not sad anymore, Robert. I'm still here. Still on watch a half-century later, trapped within the walls of this house I died in by the promise I made. But the things I've learned while waiting have brought a sense of peace.

The years have been unkind to you.

I've watched you age. The lines crept onto your face as you married that other woman, raised a houseful of sons, became a widower again. The crow's feet deepened around your eyes as you trained your gaze back into the past and played your sad songs always alone, even when surrounded by your new family.

They also aged, and left you here with a ghost you refuse to see.

I'm still young, Robert. Still carrying our daughter-to-be. In this place between the worlds, time like the sun on the summer solstice, stands still. It seems to me just days ago that we fell in love dancing the foxtrot at Hickman Hall. And wasn't it just yesterday that we were getting married at St. Thaddeus Episcopal

Church? Oh Robert, look at me. Hear me, please. Don't let the tragedy of the night I died blot out the triumphs of our days of revelry.

In ancient Rome, the longest day of the year was sacred to Juno, the goddess of women, marriage, childbirth. It was a popular time for weddings, for it was believed that Juno would bless the union and ease the passing of newborn souls from the world of spirits into the world of flesh. Maybe the Romans, like those of us who live between the worlds, could sense the thinning of the walls that separate the living from the dead.

In the here and now of this night of the summer solstice, I reach my hand toward yours. If you would only turn toward me, meet my gaze, intertwine your fingers with mine, we could breach those walls and make contact.

But your whole focus remains on the piano keys.

It won't be long before you shed your skin and join us, my love. The fiery spirit that is our unborn baby girl will finally separate from her mother, and the three of us will move on into the next world together. I catch glimpses of that world from time to time, superimposed against the night sky like the aurora borealis—crackles of color and whispers of light amid a cacophony of sound like a thousand orchestras playing jubilant chords all at once and forever.

For tonight, though, the melancholy notes of "Clair de Lune" swell out of the piano at your fingertips and sweep across the moonlit living room to fade into the dark. Tonight, as I lean toward the warmth of your body but feel only heartbreak, I promise to keep my watch.

Malachite Cross and the Seven Sisters

Malachite Cross and the Seven Sisters

Jerry Craven

A malachite cross here surfing with grace
and bathed in a star's yellow light
is stretching out time and purpling space
in defining the shape of a night.

This painting with those Seven Sisters invites
me to a childhood sky close to Rio
el Tigre and closer to our El Tigrito
backyard water tower. Carl's

Seven Sisters burned warm in the night,
standing together, Carl said, like the dipper
now in this strange malachite art.
As he spoke of planets and the Pleiades,
my finger traced his words through those
sizzling stars until finding made the Sisters
mine to hold forever in my racing heart.

Light-years from that childhood, I hear Carl,
a man wise from Time and shaking slow
to conjure words of mourning for one sister,
then telling a plan to write another book.

My promise to help draws a dark look
from the lady who knows him best. Your brother,
she tells me aside, cannot hold a pen.
Those fingers have forgotten all keyboards,
and the hospice nurse helps him endure his pain.
He has already written his last book.

But I know a plan can help shape the night
like the malachite cross coloring space, defining
time and truth for all we've seen in our light.

The Woman Who Never Smiled

The Woman Who Never Smiled

Terry Dalrymple

I first saw the woman who never smiled at a small, modest resort on the Gulf Coast. I had recently retired from a university, and I wanted to treat myself to something special. My first evening there, I sat in the bar sipping Wild Turkey with a splash when she walked in. Early thirties, beautiful. She moved like water: liquid, flowing, and natural. She sat in a corner booth alone. After greeting her, the waiter brought her a glass of white wine. She sipped her wine, read a book, and looked so very, very sad. What, I wondered, would make such a lovely young woman look that sad?

I had intended to have the one drink and then move to the restaurant for the Catch-of-the-Day but, fascinated by this stunning woman and her sadness, I ordered a second bourbon and watched her. If someone passed her booth, she would glance up and then straight back down at her book. One man about her age appeared to make a special trip to her corner. He stopped, smiled at her, said something, and extended his hand. She looked up, eyes and face reflecting only grief, spoke briefly, and looked back down, ignoring the hand he had offered. He shrugged and returned to his table.

Her fingers were long and slender, and her delicate wrist moved smoothly as she raised her glass to her lips and tilted it to get the last sip. She fished some bills out of a small purse and left them on the table. As she walked out, I squinted to see the book title, but the hand that clutched it covered all but "Finding" and "verse." I imagined she preferred sad poems, and two lines from an Edna St. Vincent Millay poem came back to me:

I only know that summer sang in me
A little while, that in me sings no more.

* * *

The woman who never smiled had been a girl who smiled enthusiastically and often, at everything and nothing at all. In college, though, she felt lonely and began to smile less. Then she met the boy of her dreams. He was handsome, gentlemanly, sensitive, kind, and generous, and she fell for him passionately. Her smiles returned, often mixed with laughter. They spoke of marrying after graduation. What few hours she spent alone, she spent daydreaming about the wedding and about their whole wonderful lifetime together.

But over time the young man fell in, as the saying goes, with the wrong crowd. He often opted to drink with his so-called friends while she sat in a corner feeling blue about what had become of him. He drank far too much. The day she confronted him seriously about his drinking and his dismissive attitude toward her, he told her she was a prude, told her she didn't know how to celebrate the freedom of college life, told her to shut up and leave him alone. He might as well have punched her in the face, she thought. That would have been less painful. She stopped going anywhere with him, and he didn't ask why. And she stopped smiling. She sat in her apartment, sad and alone, waiting for him to call. He never did, and then he quit school and disappeared without a word. She never smiled again.

But that's just a story I told myself after the first time I saw the woman who never smiled. I don't believe it. It has no smack of truth. It's too common, too trite for the lovely, graceful woman who never smiled.

* * *

I did not see the woman who never smiled again until my second evening. I spent the day lazily, wandering the beach and reading by the swimming pool. At five, I visited the bar but did not spot her there. I took a drink out to the gulf-view patio. She wasn't there. The warm, salty breeze reminded me of childhood vacations to the gulf, and I sat to enjoy it and nurse my drink.

In the restaurant, I saw her. As in the bar the previous night, she occupied a back corner. I spotted an empty table adjacent to hers and asked the hostess if I might sit there. When a waitress seated me, the woman looked up. I smiled and nodded. She offered the hint of a nod but no smile and then looked back down at her plate of food, shrimp scampi and linguine. She ate in small, delicate bites. I ordered blackened red snapper and a glass of Riesling. I snuck glances at her but never saw her offer anyone passing anything but tight lips and sad eyes. I was close enough that I could see clearly the title of the book she had placed on her table's outer end: *Finding Our Place in the Universe*. So, not verse but universe. Was it a self-help book? An astronomy book? Something else?

I wondered if she might speak with me. She had spoken only briefly with that man the night before, and that appeared to be a dismissal. Perhaps an old retired man would not be a threat. She dabbed her lips with a napkin she lifted gracefully from her lap. She laid the napkin on the table and motioned for the check. After paying, she arose, and I arose, too, hoping the move looked nonchalant. I pointed to her book. "Looks interesting." She nodded. Closer then, I could read the smaller print at the bottom of the book cover: "How We Discovered Laniakea, the Milky Way's Home." Astronomy, then. The author was a woman. But the woman I wondered about was the one holding the book, who spoke only to excuse herself and walk away. In her voice, as in her eyes, I sensed Gerard Manley Hopkins's plea, let me "not live this tormented mind / With this tormented mind tormenting yet."

* * *

The woman who never smiled—let's call her Astra—had been happy enough in childhood, the happiest when she sat in her yard at night gazing at the moon and stars. She yearned to know all about them. From grade school through high school, she read every book about outer space in the schools' libraries. Some did not satisfy because they were oversimplified. Others were too technical for her to fully comprehend, and those disappointed because they ignored what she perceived as the magic of the cosmos.

During her last two years of high school, too naïve to understand that wanting and achieving could be two different things entirely, she dreamed of enrolling in a university astronomy program and eventually becoming an astronaut. She hoped to spacewalk among the stars. But though she was capable in all subjects, she quickly lost interest in most, her mind wandering instead across the night sky, its splendor, its mystery. She finished high school with average grades. Additionally, she discovered that both her desired major and, most especially, NASA's requirements consisted wholly of science, technology, engineering, and mathematics courses. No magic and mystery. So she skipped college and went to work for a chain department store. And she never smiled again.

That's better, I think, closer, perhaps, to truth. Her story must be something about lost

33

hope and a stifling of romantic visions of wonder, mystery, and magic. Still, she strikes me as far more capable than the girl with average grades who was so naïve about her dream job. It's more than that, deeper than that. I'm sure of it.

* * *

On my third and last day at the resort I saw her in the lobby reading her book when I entered to grab the morning paper. Passing near her chair, I said good morning, and without looking up she responded in kind. So, a nod and an "Excuse me" the day before and a morning greeting my last day. Perhaps I could still find out more about her before leaving the resort. Around noon I spotted her in the restaurant eating a salad but had no opportunity to approach her. She wore a white linen dress that complemented her lightly tanned skin. Later, when I went for a short swim in the warm Gulf waters, I recognized that dress as she walked far down the beach. I did not see her at dinner, but on a stroll after I had eaten I saw her sitting on the steps of a boardwalk that led to the beach.

Hands in pockets, I approached casually. I offered a good evening to her. She set the book down and said, "Good evening," polite but still sad. I asked if she studied astronomy. She looked up at a sliver of moon and scanned the night full of stars. "Casually," she said. I said the sky was beautiful and she nodded. "Always." Her tone clearly expressed both sincerity and melancholy. Her brief answers did not encourage conversation. At a loss for anything else to say I mentioned that I'd be going home the next day. She nodded. "So will I." Did she live nearby? I asked. Instead of answering, she arose and walked about ten feet down the boardwalk. She leaned on the rail and stared again at the sky, silent.

The Gulf breeze fluttered the hem of her dress just above her knees, and I sat admiring all her grace and beauty, which seemed so contradictory of the deep sadness reflected in her face. After a couple minutes she said, still gazing skyward, "No, not nearby. Far, far away." How far? I wondered but did not ask. Did she, as Wordsworth writes, "cometh from afar," and did she arrive "Trailing clouds of glory?" And did she mourn her loss of "the glory and the dream" out there among those bright stars in an otherwise dark sky?

* * *

Let's say that like most newborns Astra cried as soon as she was delivered. But unlike most newborns, she didn't stop crying until she was just over a year old. Doctors were no help to her weary, frustrated parents, for they found no medical explanation for baby's complaint. And then, a few days after turning one, Astra abruptly stopped crying. She never cried again. When her mother rocked her and sang to her, the girl lay peacefully in the woman's arms and stared up at her with large, dark eyes. But she never smiled.

Let's say that as she grew she became obsessed with the sky, with stars and planets, with the entire galaxy and whatever stretched beyond it across the universe. When her parents checked on her before they went to bed, they would often find that she had crawled out of her upstairs bedroom window to sit on the roof and study the starlit sky. One particular night when Astra was seven, her mother crawled out to join her. They sat silently, eyes wandering the space above, until her mother asked the question she had yearned to ask since the girl was born. Why so sad?

Astra shrugged, then said, "I miss home." Her mother observed that where they were was her home. "No, I mean my first home." Mom played along, asked where that was.

Astra pointed straight up. "There," she said.

She was smart and learned quickly. Let's say she did go to college, got a degree in business management, went to work as a clerk at Neiman Marcus, and over time worked her way up until she managed the Women's Clothing Department. All this despite never smiling. It seems feasible for a bright, lovely, graceful woman. And so does this: Over a long weekend, she drove to Port Aransas, where she stayed in a modest resort. She spent her time reading, walking on the beach, and scanning the night skies. On her last night there she sat on the steps of a boardwalk, read for a time, then rose to stroll the arched walkway. At the far end, where she should have disappeared on the walkway's descent to the beach, instead she stepped out into the air and walked to the stars she had admired so long. She went home, and once there she smiled.

That is a true story. I tell it to myself often. And I believe it.

It was the twenty-ninth of December in the year 2009, a day I thought was perfect.
Andrew Geyer

3. Small Creatures

Moth Landing

Moth Landing

Andrew Geyer

I heard the rain last night. Whispering on the roof like the sighs of a hundred lovers known and left behind, the rain returned after a long dry winter. I opened the windows and let the scent of spring fill my little house near Medicine Creek. And from that moment to this, as the storm rumbled in across the Wichita Mountains, and rolled across Lake Lawtonka to shudder my walls before fading away across the Southwest Oklahoma plains, I knew that the moths would come.

I've always known things.

Since my earliest girlhood, growing up with my Kiowa grandmother in this house on the outskirts of Lawton, Oklahoma, I've caught glimpses of future moments. Like clips from home movies of me not yet filmed, they flicker and fade. Ephemeral. Such is the nature of premonitions, at least for me. The story of my life is a cautionary tale of warnings forgotten or ignored.

But soon, despite everything that has come and gone, the sun will rise on the first day of spring. My pain will end. I'll grow wings, and the moths will lead me away to a new beginning.

With the exception of a slow-motion train wreck of a marriage to the foreman of a ranch outside Elk City, I've spent my whole adult life in Lawton, serving booze. I was a cocktail waitress until two babies in three years with the ranch foreman rearranged the shape of my curves. I've been tending bar since the divorce. Two life lessons I learned in thirty years on the clock with the drinking public: an intimate appreciation of the word *irony*, and the inestimable value of lists.

It wasn't until the cancer, though, that I learned the art of making my lists ironical. They say that irony is a sign of intelligence and creativity, and I think that's true. As an example, here's a little something I've been working on while I savor the scent of the rain:

1. Indian weds cowboy;
2. Bartending alcoholic
3. Dies on the first day of spring.

It's not quite a traditional haiku, but it captures the arc of my life.

The astronomical term for the day that is dawning, at last, is the Vernal Equinox. I think a better word is *magical*—the eastern horizon giving birth once again to the season of spring. Blood red brightens into orange, then yellow. And the new spring sun, rising like a sideways rainbow, backlights the moths on my window sill: gypsy, ruby maple, cecropia, luna. One moth each for the sacred medicines: tobacco, sweetgrass, sage, cedar. Eight delicate antennae, eight arching wings etched in silhouette by the sunrise onto the palette of my screen.

I know that the gypsy moth is the soul of my Kiowa grandmother returned, like the spring, to guide me to the light. The other three are the spirits of ancestors come to ease my passing from this world of sorrows into blossom-strewn plains of green.

Metamorphosis is a part of moth's magic.

I remember my grandmother telling me so, her voice soft and certain. "The egg symbolizes the birth of an idea, the larvae the foundation, the chrysalis the manifestation of change. The growth of wings," she said, "symbolizes taking flight into uncharted territory." After a life spent in Lawton, uncharted territory sounds awfully good to me. Here are some facts I learned as the last dry winter dragged on and on:

1. The two main types of cervical cancer are squamous cell carcinoma and adeno carcinoma;
2. Small cell cervical cancer, which is also called small cell neuroendocrine carcinoma, is a rare and aggressive type with a five-year survival rate of only 15% when diagnosed at Stage 4;
3. It affects fewer than three in every 100 women diagnosed;
4. I am one of those three.

But as the first rays of spring sun warm my face through the window, everything is light and life. On the far side of the screen, the moths are afire in a kaleidoscope of colors. On the inside, the bright orange oxymorphone tablets glow like a dozen tiny suns in my grandmother's sky blue ceramic bowl. I wash down the first three with a deep draught of red wine from the glass at my side. Then I wash down three more.

It's almost time to take flight.

The sun has risen already over the ranch outside Elk City that I returned to last week to say goodbye to my younger son. The older boy lives in Tulsa, last I heard. We haven't spoken since his father kicked me off the place. But here in Lawton, the sun is a yellow-white halfcircle against the jagged black sawblade of the Wichita Mountains.

Now the moths are stretching their wings. And multiplying. Four become eight. Then the eight double in number. The sixteen double again, and again, to sixty-four, and again. Until there are too many to count, moths of all textures and colors, white witch moths and eyed hawkmoths and yellow woolly bear moths and ruby tiger moths and species of moths I cannot name, stretching up into infinity outside my window like a living bridge.

When the half-sun turns full, I'll wash down six more pills.

But already, I feel the tingle of new growth in my shoulder blades. My metamorphosis is underway. A green season beckons, and my new wings will soon be strong enough to bear me away. My arrival will be as a moth landing.

Uncle Marvin Smoked a Worm

Uncle Marvin Smoked a Worm

Jerry Craven

Once I awoke in my Amarillo home to the sound of a worm walking around in my room. Dizzy from sleep, I listened to what sounded like a quick, sharp scratch on a screen, so I turned on the light to locate the noise. And there it was, the size of my grandmother's centipede, the one that leaped upon her from a woodpile behind her Friendswood home.

The worm wrapped itself around her wrist three times, so she had to grab it with finger and thumb to tug its needle feet from her skin. She flipped it to the ground and chopped it into wriggling and dying parts with her axe.

My nighttime worm crawled and scratched on a newspaper left on the floor. Not having an axe handy—though the image of Grandmother using her axe on the worm came to me—I whacked the centipede several times with a shoe, then jerked some Kleenex from a box, seized the worm, and carried it into the bathroom to flush it away. As I released it, a faint stinging of fingers reminded me of Grandmother's centipede tracks on her arm, red spots like a bracelet that became as inflamed and infected as the places on her thumb and finger, the wounds of battle in killing the hundred-legged worm. My nighttime paper scratcher had nailed me through the Kleenex, and later in the night I dreamed of Grandmother's bracelet.

In Japan, my daughter assures me, worms similar to American nightcrawlers come to the surface after a rain to blow long, moaning love songs through their wormy mouths, a sound made for attracting a mate. Singing worms, she calls them. Never except in dreams have I seen a singing worm, and mine were huge like the ones people learned to ride in Herbert's Dune novels. Such worms as sing in my dreams run blubbery and stupid in dry desert sand, unlike the wet Borneo jungle worm I once found while awake.

Charles, the English name of an Iban tribesman hired to take me to Bat Cave deep in the jungle, stopped after we waded through a creek, a feeder for the Skrang River. "We must take off our shoes," he said, "to see if anyone is in there."

I sat to remove my shoes and found it crawling its ponderous way across one sock, that sperm-shaped leech as long as my thumb, a worm that writhed with great energy when Charles pinched it between sticks.

I have seen leeches in Venezuelan as well as Asian jungles, and once I found them in an Ohio field after a summer rain when I set out to gather fish bait, worms called nightcrawlers, though I picked them up during the day. The nightcrawlers surfaced not to sing but to escape drowning in soggy soil. In several puddles were leeches, which I prodded with a stick, flipping them over to look at their suction cups, then congratulating myself for not donating blood to any of them.

In the Borneo jungle, I asked my guide, "If it had stuck to my skin, how would you remove it?"

"With tobacco," Charles said, "or poison."

"But isn't tobacco poison?"

"That's what I mean." Charles gave me a sidelong look as if I were a simpleton or a child. But I knew tobacco isn't poisonous to all worms, for Uncle Marvin found some that ate tobacco. I was a child when I watched him rummage through an old car he had stolen and parked in the backyard of our Port Arthur home. Under the seat he found the remains of a Baby Ruth, several pennies, bobby pins, a paperback with its cover ripped away, and an ancient package of Lucky Strikes. It looked water-stained and maimed, but that didn't stop Uncle Marvin from ripping into it. "Smokes," he said with enthusiasm. In mere seconds a disreputable-looking bent cigarette hung from his lower lip while he pulled a lighter from his jeans pocket.

"But, Uncle Marvin," I pointed. "That looks like worms in your cigarette."

He lighted it, took a drag, and held the cigarette at arm's length to examine it. "Yeah?" He shrugged. "I heard of that. I heard that sometimes bugs lay eggs in old cigarettes and worms hatch out to chew on the tobacco." He took another drag. "One thing's for sure, I'm getting rid of the worms that are chawing down on the tobacco." He jerked his shoulders in laughter.

In a Venezuelan jungle I met people who ate worms. Others might call them caterpillars, but to me, fuzzy worms are still worms. I watched a jungle native wearing a blue skirt grab a caterpillar from a bush, put it into his mouth, and chew with what appeared to be gusto not unlike Uncle Marvin's enjoyment of the wormy smokes.

In my father's diamond-mining camp along the Caroni River, some locals prepared a side dish for dinner by dropping worms into hot grease, an act that frizzed off the caterpillar hair and made the worms look to a *norte americano* almost like something to eat. As a child I once awoke from a nasty dream of having to eat fried worms that, in the strange world of dreams, managed to crawl out of hot, crackling grease.

But consumption of worms is an old memory, something dredged from a childhood when I roamed what was then the wild interior of Venezuela. Perhaps today the jungle people have given up worm eating, though I doubt it.

People in Dallas certainly don't eat worms, and there's plenty there to be had, especially in the spring when fuzzy bag worms grow fat in pecan trees. They make the tree look as if it has been wounded and bandaged. People hate such worms and resort to assorted modes of violence to kill them.

My father killed the bag worms in our East Texas pecan trees by burning the nests with alcohol-soaked flaming rags attached to a pole. Such tactics, our neighbor Allen assured me, are unwise. "My uncle," he declared, "burned down two of his houses while holding flames into pecan trees too close to his roof."

I didn't believe Allen. Maybe his uncle burned down one house. But two? I figured anyone would learn from the first burnout not to go for another. My father was lucky because he never burned down a single one of our houses, though he torched bag worms each spring.

The gauzy bags always flamed in dramatic ways, and I learned early on to flee the area, for scorched as well as live worms rained upon my head if I hung around. After the burning of a spring infestation of bag worms, I had a nightmare about flaming worms crawling up my pants, setting my jeans on fire.

Outdoor worms are bad enough, but some people in Dallas have to deal with indoor worms, or so I learned when Ann told me about the wiggly critters in her carpet.

She said they surfaced from time to time, tiny, white, and hungry. Usually she found them in dark places: under an end-table, beneath chairs. The exterminator she called pulled the carpet back to show her some ragged spots where worms ate the wool. He treated the carpet, but he shook his head while doing so, and he said he couldn't guarantee his work. "Carpet worms are hard to kill," he said. Ann decided to take drastic measures to rid her house of the worms.

Maybe not so drastic as Uncle Marvin's smoking the tobacco worms or Dad's torching the bag worms, but drastic enough. After Ann told me about her cure, I dreamed of carpet worms, though mine crawled around in my hair. In the dream they were huge, but in reality the worms that once crawled on my scalp were small and white, not unlike those in Ann's rug. I was about eight years old and living in a Venezuelan village when the worms jumped me, an attack that started with a parasitic fly. I complained to my mother about an itchy spot on my head. Mom examined the spot, then whisked me into Dad's pickup. She drove me to the office of Doctor Breseño, who tisk-tisked over the spongy spot on my scalp, daubed it with alcohol on a cotton swab, and used a scalpel to nudge out three tiny worms. "*Gusanos del monte*," he said. Jungle worms. Usually, he said, the fly lays her eggs on goats or donkeys, but sometimes they choose humans. Mom almost went into hysterics, but Doctor Breseño merely shrugged. "The worms do little damage," he said.

At first the scalp worms didn't alarm me, but, later, after I told the kids in the oil company camp's school about what Doctor Breseño found on my head, I came to hate those worms when kids called me "maggoty-headed."

The worms Ann had to deal with ruined her carpet. Never mind, she told me, that it was a beautiful Persian work of art, one that looked terrific in her home. The worms had to go. So she rolled up the carpet and dragged it into the alley behind her house where, she figured, the city trash collectors would haul it away.

But they took no notice of the rug, and it sat in the alley through a rainstorm. When she told me about the soggy and rolled up carpet, the image reminded me of a candy bar I once bought from a vending machine.

The wrapper looked wet and stained, likely a result of a leaky roof over the vending machine. It sat in the faculty lounge of a small East Texas college. I sat at one of the tables in the lounge and poked half-heartedly at the wrapper, knowing there was no way I would eat the candy inside. Then the college dean walked in, and I decided to take the opportunity to complain about the condition of the faculty lounge. "Look at this mess," I said, and ripped away the wrapper from the candy.

The results were better than I hoped, for the little chocolate roll was writhing alive with small worms.

White ones like those Dr. Breseño once removed from my scalp. Nasty-looking ones like those in Uncle Marvin's cigarette. Tiny ones like those in Ann's soggy carpet lying in the alley behind her home.

Ann made some phone calls and discovered that the city trash folk would haul away the carpet, but it had to be on the curb in front of her house, not in the alley. By then, rain water added so much weight to the rug that she could no longer tug it around without help. So she tied a rope around one end of the carpet and secured the rope to the bumper of her SUV. Her cinching the rope to the rug brought some of the worms to the surface, but she never flinched.

Why should she? Though she is an elegant and pretty woman, petite and always well dressed, she isn't one to flinch over any of nature's creatures, for she is an artist who draws plants and insects. She looks at critters in nature with an eye for detail better than that of any camera lens. So she wasn't particularly bothered when dealing with carpet worms. A trail of writhing worms littered the alley and street when she dragged the rug behind her car.

After hearing the story I had an uncomfortable night from dreaming of Ann's car pulling a giant candy bar, wet and covered with the very worms that the dean had dismissed with a wave of his hand.

"Even the best grocery stores sometimes have to deal with corrupted produce," the dean declared, and he took some coins from a pocket, dropped them into the vending machine and pulled out another bar of candy. "Try this one," he said and tossed it to me.

"Thanks," I said. "But I wouldn't eat this on a bet." I put the candy on the table in front of me.

"I know someone who would," the dean said.

"Yeah?" I thought of Uncle Marvin.

The dean picked up the candy bar. "I would." He dropped the candy into his shirt pocket, winked, and left.

The nasty candy still sat wormy on the table in front of me, and I winced at the sight, for it called to mind others, carpet worms, *gusanos del monte*, and the worst ones: those in Uncle Marvin's rotten smokes.

Alexandra looked disappointed. 'You're not here for the march, are you?' Her voice carried a hard edge of accusation.

Jerry Craven

Lepidopterophobia

Lepidopterophobia

Terry Dalrymple

The window was open just enough to let in the cool night air. Unfortunately, it was also open just enough to let in two moths. They wasted no time fluttering up inside the lamp shade of my reading light by the window. Camille would be home soon, and I had to ditch those damn moths fast.

Camille suffered from lepidopterophobia. If she returned home to see moths in the house, she would panic, convinced as she was that butterflies' and moths' sole Satanic purpose on this earth was to fly into her mouth, settle in her throat, and choke her to death. Irrational fears like that seemed ridiculous to me, and in our early dating life I teased her about it. Once, on a picnic, I said, as a joke, "There's a butterfly in your hair." She frantically slapped her head and ran erratically, blindly, screaming hysterically the whole time. Her behavior was incredibly embarrassing to me, and I never teased her again.

She had on many occasions threatened me with bodily harm if I ever opened our only unscreened window. Which happened to be the window by my favorite reading chair. The screen was missing when we bought the house, our first. I had been promising ever since to replace the screen, and much as I loved my new bride, I considered phobias inane. It's possible that was the reason for my sloth in getting round to the replacement.

Still, that evening when the moths came in, I knew I had to work fast to get them out. Earlier, after a light supper of chicken salad sandwiches and veggie chips, she had a hankering for chocolate ice cream. "Sounds good," I said. "I'll zip to the store."

She kissed me lightly. "You're my prince. But it was my idea. I'll go." As she gathered her purse and keys, I settled in my reading chair with *Time* magazine and a little Maker's over one ice cube. Open windows sounded good, so when her headlights faded down the block, I raised the screenless pane a few inches, and the moths swooped in.

I eased slowly from the chair, crept around it, and peered up into the lamp shade. One moth flapped furiously, beating itself against the bulb. The other rested calmly on the inner wall of the shade. Both were brownish-gray and couldn't have been more than a quarter inch long. How in the world could Camille look at them and see monsters? I cupped my hand, moved it slowly toward the resting Mothra, and clamped my hand over it loosely so as not to crush it. Its wings beat against my palm and fingers. I thrust my hand out the window to release it. By then, it lay motionless on my palm. I tipped my hand and it fell, apparently lifeless, into the Nandina shrub below the window. I guess my fist hadn't been as loose as I thought.

I whirled toward the lamp in time to see the other dusty-winged beast spiral up and out of the lamp shade. It bounced a clumsy zigzag pattern, clearly headed toward our bedroom, where a bedside lamp was shining.

"No!" I yelled and sprinted in its direction. Just as its spastic flapping delivered it within inches of the bedroom door, I lunged for it, missed, and fell spread-eagle onto the floor. Every psi of air stored in my lungs whooshed out at once. Even so, I rolled over to see that I had redirected the moth, which now seemed more or less aimed at the kitchen, where an overhead light glowed brightly. Gasping for breath, I pushed to my feet and stumbled after it. Open-mouth gasping, I swatted at it as it entered the kitchen. It swooped in front of my face as I sucked in a large lungful of air, and in it went, over my tongue and down my throat. Well, that was one way to get rid of it. I smiled at the thought. But when I turned to leave the kitchen, I felt what seemed to be wings beating against my trachea. I shook my head hard to eject that thought. Suddenly, I couldn't breathe. Panicked, I bent over the sink and rammed my finger into my mouth, hoping to gag myself. That's when I heard Camille enter the front door.

I couldn't hack up Satan incarnate and run the risk that Camille would see it. In that case, I'd have to confess to opening the window, and I'd be risking serious bodily harm from her. I spun around as she entered with a huge smile and held up a plastic bag with a pint of Haggen-Dazs nestled inside. Then she looked at me and frowned.

"My God," she said. "You look awful. What's wrong?"

I made a grunting noise and pointed to my chest. "Coughing fit," I croaked.

"I'll get you some water."

"Drink," I managed and staggered toward the living room. Maybe, I thought, the Maker's would not only wash the moth down but kill it from alcohol poisoning. Plus, I needed to get that window closed.

I slid the window closed in time, and when she re-entered the room I downed the Maker's and swallowed hard. The blockage slipped from my throat. I smiled. "Better," I said. "Let's have ice cream."

Camille did the scooping and filled our bowls generously. But by the time she set them on the table, I felt a little ill. It started with a vague but irritating tickle in my gut. I tried passing it off as psychosomatic, but the sensation increased until I was convinced that somehow that damned moth was still alive and flapping down there in my belly.

"You're looking pale again," Camille said. "You sure you're okay?"

Bile rose in my throat. "Maybe not. Excuse me."

Speed-walking got me to the bathroom in time to close and lock the door, bend over the toilet bowl, and heave. I flushed simultaneously because I hated to look at my own vomit. I swear I felt that moth coming up and out, wings still beating, along with partially digested chicken salad and veggie chips. But I had flushed too quickly to confirm that the beast swirled into the sewer line.

I rinsed my mouth and washed my face, and as I dried off, a terrifying notion struck. What if that creature had escaped the gaping mouth of the toilet? What if, at that moment, it lurked behind the shower curtain, dripping with bits of my expulsion. I crept to the curtain, my palms already sweaty, my face feeling prickly and hot. I pulled the curtain back just a crack, ready to bolt if that bastard flew toward my face. I saw nothing and breathed a heavy sigh of relief. I washed my face again.

When I entered the kitchen, Camille looked up, concerned. "Are you okay, baby?"

"I am now. But I think I'll skip the ice cream." I deposited my bowl in the freezer and sat across from her while she finished hers. "Do you remember those Monarchs last fall?"

She swallowed a spoonful of Rocky Road. "Don't remind me." She scrunched her face and shuddered violently. "God, there were so many."

"It's almost fall again." Goosebumps rose on my arms. "I think I'll replace that living room screen tomorrow."

She picked up her empty bowl, blew me a kiss, and stepped to the sink.

47

4. The Colors of Carnival

How You Say Home

How You Say Home

Andrew Geyer

1. *Aiken, SC: August 2019*

It's your first official day. Having been lured back to SC from the Lone Star State by the offer of higher pay, a reduced course load, and tenure, you park your battered SUV among the shiny gas-sipping hybrids in the faculty section of the B Lot and walk through the pine tree shade, past the azaleas on the quad, and up to your office where the newly installed placard reads: *Dr. Joe Jasmine, Chair, Department of Languages, Literatures, and Cultures*. After not too long a while, the professor who occupies the office next door pokes his head in and reintroduces himself (as English Department Chair, he served as the non-LLC faculty member on the search committee that hired you). You exchange the requisite pleasantries and agree to get a beer in the historic downtown after work. Then he looks at you intently. "It's ironical, right?"

"Ironical?" You glance quickly down to make sure that, in the rush to leave the house amid the flutter of first-day jitters, you didn't accidently slip on the *Moana* necktie your 3-year-old daughter Beatrice (with a little help from her mother Sara) gave you on your last birthday.

"Your bumper sticker," he says, the ghost of a smile playing expectantly across his lips. "The Texas thing. It's ironical, right?"

"My . . . bumper." Then it strikes you. Literally the last thing you did before following the moving van east was paste a bumper sticker onto the hindquarters of your mesquite-thorn-scratched gas-guzzler: AMERICAN BY BIRTH, TEXAN BY THE GRACE OF GOD. "Oh that," you say.   "No. It's not ironical."

The smile fades from your colleague's face as he vacates your office. But to his credit (although he is the scion of a deep-blue state and more than a bit of a blue blood), the two of you do go and drink that beer. Afterward, you agree to do happy hour again next week. But your blue-blooded, blue-state colleague and tentative friend is still mystified by the *Texas thing*.

The honest truth is that you are too. Despite the bumper sticker.

Your relationship with your native state lies at the heart of everything you've ever written, everything you are. And yet, bumper sticker aside, you don't really even know what to call that relationship—what label to put on it.

Conflicted is too vague. *Love-hate* gets the evolution of your feelings exactly backwards. Maybe *hate-love*.

Is that how you say home?

2. *Frio County, TX: 1973-1983*

A barbed wire fence separated the weaning lot from the backyard of the ranch house your father and mother built. The cattle pens lay on the far side of the weaning lot, and the water lot surrounded the pens. Another barbed wire fence divided the front yard from the horse lot and stable. The white brick ranch house stood on the highest hill on the Home Place (which everyone but your family had called the Jasmine Place for three generations) and commanded a view that stretched for miles. But the only sights to see from the wrap-around porch were horses and cows, mesquite and cactus, plowed fields alternating with pastures of coastal Bermuda, the hay barn, the cross-fences of other ranches in the far distance. The nearest neighbors lived more than a mile away. There was nothing much to do outside of the endless daily round of ranch work and chores, and you hated it all with a passion that seems, after the long passage of years, almost impossible to explain—much less capture with a single word.

But there was *Christmas*:

3 am, and you're kneeling with your arms shoulder-deep in the uterus of a heifer trying desperately to birth her first calf. Her hindquarters are covered in shit and blood and God knows what else, and so are your sodden clothes. You're searching deep inside her for a pair of forelegs to attach the padded chain in your hands to, securely enough so that the come-along your father will use to pull the calf won't just tear off two unborn hooves. It's not the first time you've knelt so, nor will it be the last, and the fact that it's Christmas Eve makes no difference. Since the onset of your big teenage growth spurt, you've been graced with the longest arms on a ranch whose lifeblood is a cow-calf operation—and the calf crop must be born.

And *August*:

Mid-afternoon, the temperature 105 degrees in the shade. You are not in the shade. Peanut vines in the field you're working in have run too far across the between-row spaces for the cultivator blades, and so (peanuts being the cash crop) you trudge, the hoe sweat-slick in your hands, through the middle of a 120-acre field, gazing through the heat waves at the bright blue water jug that shimmers in the far distance. You bend, yank a stubborn-rooted carelessweed from among the vines at your feet, slog on. Poking up through the deep green peanut leaves, you count the gray-green patches of carelessweeds that lie between you and your next drink of cold water: one, two, three, four, five . . .

And *ice*:

First light. The coming sun crimsons the frost that covers everything but the cattle and you. The task at hand?   Cracking the crust off the 35-foot circular cattle trough so the cows can drink. You take the hatchet and cattle prod from behind the seat of your rusted-out old ranch truck, crack a 3-inch ring of ice from around the concrete edge of the trough with the hatchet, haul out the clear jagged shards. Next you smash up the 2-inch thick sheet across the middle with the cattle prod, cracking and hooking and hauling out chunks until the surface of the trough is clear and you're half-soaked and your hands are numb. Then you shoulder your way through the gentle black cows, climb into the truck, head to your first-period Spanish class at the high school in town.

At the age of eighteen, you couldn't get away from Southwest Texas, and from that life on the land, fast enough. *Escape* was the only word that came to mind as you loaded the last of your stuff onto the back of the truck and lit out for Austin.

3. *Austin, TX / Columbia, SC / Austin, TX: 1989-2006*

After two undergraduate degrees at the University of Texas, you headed to South Carolina for the first time to earn a master's degree and a doctorate—and more importantly, to begin the expansion of horizons (and accompanying diminution of obstacles) that would remake your life. You canoed rivers. Climbed mountains. Studied *The Quixote* in the original Spanish. Bodysurfed.

You lived in ramshackle houses with a wild assortment of friends and lovers, fellow travelers all, doing and thinking and feeling the same things as you. You met and married your first wife. You became a father. And when you held your newborn son against your chest for the first time, and said the word "Jacob," you discovered in your heart of hearts a kind of love that you never dreamed was possible—and for which neither the Spanish nor the English language contains a term.

After fits and starts and side-trails (and adjuncting what felt like a thousand classes), you landed a full-time teaching job at Austin Community College, a couple of hundred miles away from the ranch you grew up on, selling the contents of your head instead of scratching a living with your hands out of a semi-desert chunk of dust and rock and scrub brush. It was the polar opposite of life on the Home Place. But as the years in Austin stretched out, you visited—and saw things change. Every time you returned, driving southwest to San Antonio and on through the rolling hills of cactus and mesquite, there were fewer cross-fences. Each time you sat with your mother and father on the wrap-around porch, surrounded by the fruits of their labor, there looked to be fewer of those fruits than before. Your conversations centered on which farm and ranch support programs were being scaled back this year, or cut altogether; which of the family ranches that you grew up working cattle on during the fall and spring roundups had been foreclosed on, or had sold out to big beef operations.

Then your father died face-down in a field of coastal Bermuda. He'd been dead for hours from the massive heart attack when your mother found him among grazing black cows. But it wasn't until the graveside service that it really hit you: a way of life was passing. Not just a set of customs, but a way of seeing the world, and being in it, that reached back to the days of the open range. The people who had lived that life were leaving it behind—whether the way your father did, or by a forced sale. On the Home Place, the hay barn was mostly empty; the cattle herd had dwindled; the horses had been sold. Still, a week after the funeral, you left your mother to handle the ranch alone. The truth was that your life in Austin was falling apart, and you were too busy trying to hold the pieces together to think about anything else.

The week after you got back your wife told you, just before she walked out the front door, that she'd never really loved you. So you sold your house, quit your job (and the side-gig that paid the mortgage), took your son, and moved back to the ranch you grew up on.

Broken was the way you said "home" for a long, dark time.

4. Frio County, TX: 2007-2019
You spent the next twelve years learning how to rebuild.

The ranch first. You, your son Jacob, and your mother gave all that you had to give and then some: patching fences, replanting overgrazed pastures, refilling the haybarn, restocking the cattle herd.

Family next. Buoyed by the continuing revival of the Home Place, you met and somehow managed to marry a gorgeous dirty-blonde with eyes the color of the Brazos river running clear in a limestone bed. Sara. The love of your life. You first laid eyes on her in the King William Historic District in San Antonio, hugging an ugly old scandal of a house as though it were a mansion. You walked up, introduced yourself, and invited her out to see the ranch: "an even bigger fixer-upper," you said, "than the one in your arms." In addition to her 5-year-old sprite of a daughter, Ariel; and Jacob, with whom ranch life agreed; your splendid blend grew to include a son named Ben and a daughter named Beatrice. As you held them close to your heart, each in turn, you rediscovered that love for which neither Spanish nor English contains a term; and you built a house big enough to hold it all—plus a cat and a dog.

Career last.   You published a book.   Got a tenure-track job at UTSA. Another book followed. Enough to keep the ranch afloat and the family together.

Then came the day you found your mother lying on the kitchen floor of the house you grew up in—unconscious, barely breathing, the left side of her face twisted, the green-and-white checkered linoleum covered in the contents of her bladder and bowels. She never came back to herself, although you spared no expense trying to make that happen. Two strokes later, you laid her to rest in the family plot beside your father.

Later that evening, you sat on the wrap-around porch with Sara and drank wine the color of the last sliver of sun dying behind the line of hills that marked your childhood horizon. She took your hand, and you listened together to the sounds of night slowly falling: the wind soughing in the mesquites, the crickets singing in the near distance, the faraway coyotes barking at the moon.

A clear-headed look at finances the following morning made it plain that selling the ranch was the only option. The family who had owned the place next to yours for three generations offered enough to wipe the slate clean and make a new start. A job search, followed by too many long nights spent packing up the contents of two houses, left you standing on the highest hill of the ranch you grew up on and looking east as the dust of the moving van settled—and wondering how you could possibly say home now.

Maybe *flight*:

Riding bareback through the soft morning air of May, running flat-out with no bridle and no bit, just the halter and the lead rope looped and tied off for reins, thick green coastal Bermuda whizzing beneath your bare feet. Except for his mane whipping back against your face, the feel of the horse charging forward between your clenched knees is like riding a rocket, a pair of shorts and a t-shirt the only things separating the two of you, the pound of his hooves ringing in your ears the only sound in the wide green world.

Or *dove stew*:

Lounging in the shade of a backyard mesquite, a shotgun across your lap and a glass of sweet iced tea nestled in the carpet grass at your feet, you scan the late September sky. It isn't long before three gray dots rise up out of a field of dark red maize and into deep blue, winging their way at forty-five miles per hour toward the water lot. You stand, hearing the high-pitched whine as they curve away, then swing the shotgun up to your shoulder, squeeze the trigger, and send the lead bird tumbling into the carpet grass ten feet from your glass of tea. By supper time, you've shot your limit. After you've cleaned them, your mother sautés the breasts with garlic and onions and tomatoes, and serves them up over rice, with homemade cornbread.

Or *learning to drive*:

Among the Indian blankets and bluebonnets that speckle the pasture red and yellow and azure, your father is teaching you to drive the rusty old ranch truck that will belong to you only after you've mastered the manual transmission. The morning is filled with lurching, clutch-jerking, engine-killing frustration on your part and white-knuckled, doorhandle-gripping resolve on his. And when you've managed at last to shift from first to second, from second to third, and back down again—and your father formally pronounces the truck to be yours—you thrust your head out the open window and howl pure freedom into the cloudless sky.

Thinking of those things, and those things only, you peeled the bumper sticker in your hands off its backing and pasted it onto the bumper of your battered SUV: AMERICAN BY BIRTH, TEXAN BY THE GRACE OF GOD.

Then you climbed into the driver's seat and, surrounded by family, headed for the last time down the long dirt road that led to the highway. Behind you, your oldest boy sat behind the wheel of the newer version of your SUV, bare of mesquite-thorn scratches but graced by the same bumper sticker. A brisk morning breeze stirred your hair, carrying with it the poignantly familiar scents of horses and cattle and freshly turned earth, and you thought about pulling over to take a last backward look. But, you remembered, the Home Place was someone else's now. Anyway, all that lay on the far side of the barbed wire fence resided inside you, and in those who rode with you. Home would come along the whole way. mMm

Make this Angel Sylvia a living and holy curanora.
Jerry Craven

The Magnificent Wink of Bird Millman

The Magnificent Wink of Bird Millman

Jerry Craven

When the mudshow came to Bridge City, I sneaked under the tent. I got away with it, mostly, and Bird Millman winked at me.

Nasty Texas mud from pig pens had soaked my shirt and trousers because the only way I could afford to admire in person Bird and her tightrope walk was to sneak in, and that meant crawling through the stinky barrier that the carnival workers shoveled along the south edge of the tent to ward off sneaking freeloaders like me.

It happened, the wink, just as Bird opened her balance umbrella. She looked down, and our eyes locked for a moment. She gave me a wonderful wink and stepped onto the tightrope.

I sat, stunned by the wink, while she walked that rope, danced on it, smiled at everyone, finished her show with a glance at me. No wink this time, just a tiny nod.

I patted my shirt pocket for the poem I had written in case there was an opportunity to hand it to Bird. It spoke of her beauty, which I had heard about but never seen, and it contained some good figurative speech—all for nothing, I realized when I patted the soggy mess in my pocket.

Mrs. Millman, Bird's mother, while standing, rode a horse bareback. She did a flip with the horse still running, and she landed on the horse without a stumble. While the crowd cheered, Bird waved, gestured for me to meet her outside the tent.

As I approached, she stepped back, one hand going to her nose. "It's the carnie's pig mud." She spoke as if apologizing.

"Hello, Bird," I said. "I'm Charlie. Because of that wink, I will be yours forever."

Her face brightened. "You're too young for me."

"I'm sixteen."

She tilted her head in surprise, put her hand on her breast. "I'm fifteen and glad that you're older than me. Can you come to the show tomorrow in Port Arthur?"

"Yes. Yes." In that moment I would have said yes if she had named London or Mexico City.

Port Arthur is home. I had borrowed Bobby Chase's Volkswagen to get to the mudshow in Bridge City. Posters around the town called it a carnival, but East Texas is mainly reclaimed swampland with mud everywhere. So we call carnivals mudshows.

"Use this to get in." She held her hand toward me. "Stay out of pig mud."

With a few fast steps, I accepted her gift, a token of some sort. Then I scrambled back, and she disappeared into the show tent.

The next morning demanded a poem about the true meaning of Bird Millman's wink. Unlike the poem ruined by pig mud, "The Magnificent Wink of Bird Millman" was excellent: no heavy rhythm, plenty of images, rhyme tucked into spots of music or silence. The grand final line promised forever love.

A risky statement, I know, but the words rang as true as her wonderful wink. I asked Danny Doyle to print the poem in calligraphy. He did it, though he smirked as he carved letters in the final line.

I scrubbed out Bobby Chase's VW, but the faint aroma of pig remained, so I thought it best not to ask again to borrow his car. Instead I walked out Procter Extension to the mudshow, which was delayed by rain. The sun set before the show opened. The warmup featured two clowns, one of them Bird's father. Bird was the main attraction.

When her moment came, she stood high on the platform, searching the audience, and somehow she located me. With a smile and a wink, she began a walk and dance across the tightrope.

Another wink! Delicious. I checked to make sure I still had her poem. At that moment I owned two glorious Bird winks. The two counterbalanced my use of the word *forever*. When we met outside the show tent, she waved toward the parking area. "Let's sit in your car. There's something exciting I want to talk about."

"I walked."

"My father's pickup, then, behind the main tent."

Bird chose the driver's side, and I sat as close to her as I dared. She laughed and slid toward me so our hips touched. Such closeness with the most beautiful girl in the world had me breathing fast and shallow, a response that embarrassed me, so I tried to hide it. I had wanted to approach the subject of my poem with smooth ease, but instead I blurted out, "I wrote a poem for you," and handed it to her.

"May I read it now?"

"Of course." I reached to help unfold the poem, but she pushed my hand away.

"It seems to be written in Chinese or Arabic." She turned the page this way and that.

"Calligraphy," I said.

"I can't read it in this dim light. I'll read it later." She pushed the poem into a tiny purse strapped to her waist. I cringed as she crumpled the poem into her purse.

Bird turned toward me, her face shining with excitement. "I have some unusual news," she said. "There's an agent coming tomorrow from Ringling Brothers and Barnum and Bailey to talk with me and my parents about our taking our acts to the bigtime three-ring circus."

"Would you go?"

"Are you kidding? Of course we would go. We have barely made a living with these little carnivals, and almost nobody has heard of us. It would be our chance to become famous and to make some big bucks."

"Then I'm happy for you. For your family. But I'll miss you." My voice broke, and I cleared my throat to hide it.

"Oh, silly boy. It isn't a done deal. We won't know until tomorrow. Here." She pressed another token into my hand. "Come see my show tomorrow in Nederland." She leaned into me and gave me a kiss on the cheek, then startled me by sliding that cheek kiss, wet and hot, across my face into a strange sloppy lip kiss. She got out of the pickup. "You better leave now," she said. "Tomorrow. Come see me tomorrow."

That night I tried for another poem, but too many feelings pushed me into numbed silence. Mainly it was that kiss that silenced me, such a kiss, two of them, one chaste and the other burning. The next morning I inventoried the signs of true courtship, the two winks, her scooting close so our hips touched, then. Then. Ah, then the two kisses, a perfect balance with the two winks. And finally I wrote a poem, though the words in it seemed to spin wildly around, knocking together within the lines, clanging between them.

Danny Doyle offered his calligraphy again, and Bobbie Chase loaned me his VW for my trip to Nederland. I turned down the calligraphy.

The day remained dry, the sky clear, and the mudshow sat on an almost dry field.

No winks from Bird during her tightrope act, and afterward we sat in the tight confines of the Volkswagen. As she got into the car, she said, "There is a bit of a bad smell in here." I sat in the driver's seat.

"Tell me about the circus agent."

"She came. She's beautiful, a trapeze artist, and a true lover of the circus. Maybe twice my age, though she looks quite young."

"Are you going?"

"Such an offer. Big pay. I'll be one of the stars and will make more money than I ever thought possible." Bird's eyes sparkled as she talked. "Dad will come as my financial manager, and we will have more than enough for Mom to retire. I'll travel all over the place. Europe. Asia. Maybe Africa. The agent said I can make extra money by walking tightropes between skyscrapers, even over rivers and gorges. The Congo River, maybe, she said. It is all so exciting—"

"When will you leave Texas?"

"Tomorrow morning."

"But what about packing for the trip?"

"We are always packed. Remember that we live on the road, remember—"

"I'll miss you." This time when my voice broke, she noticed.

"Charlie, Charlie. I'll miss you, too." She stroked my face, pulled me toward her, kissed my eyes as if to kiss away tears, though there were none.

She looked at her watch and got out of the VW.

"Did you figure out how to read the calligraphy?"

She looked puzzled, then seemed to understand. "Oh, that. Yes. It was sweet. What you wrote was sweet."

Sweet? What a phoney word. It struck me like a physical blow and I tried for a shrug.

"We'll write to each other."

"Of course we will." She gave me a tight smile and a wink, though it seemed clipped, cold and hard.

As I drove away I realized we had not exchanged addresses, and I told myself the omission was deliberate.

I guess I was a dirty dog for about three months, and let me tell you, it wasn't fun.
Terry Dalrymple

How Millard Mack Became Crippled

How Millard Mack Became Crippled

Terry Dalrymple

Millard Mack stood six feet, five inches tall and lived in a ramshackle house near the county line eleven miles north of Phlattsland, Texas, where he farmed cotton. One year, fascinated by little people because of his late, large mother's desire to be one, he went in search of a circus, where he meet Teensy Folger. He removed his gimme cap, bowed, and said, "Will you marry me?"

As it happened, Teensy, who stood only three feet, two inches tall, had long been fascinated by tall people. She said, "Yes, I will." And that is, perhaps, where the story of Millard Mack's becoming crippled begins.

Some years after they married, Teensy heard about the Grand Opening Extravaganza of BIG's Little Store in Phlattsland, and she told Millard they should go. The store was the first modernized grab-and-go shop in Phlattsland, and it was named after William Irving Gragg, who had always gone by Billy and so named the store BIG's Little Store, sure that BIG's was better than WIG's and pleased with himself for coming up with the ironic—or oxymoronic (he wasn't sure which)—store name.

Millard Mack allowed as how he saw no point in attending "a circus at a little convenient store."

Teensy corrected him, explaining that it was a *convenience* store, before crossing her arms, scowling and averring that she would go to BIG's Little Store's Grand Opening Extravaganza with or without him. He said, "Without." She huffed and said,"Fine."

Thus, on the day of BIG's Little Store's Grand Opening Extravaganza she clambered up into her early-model Taurus, which Millard Mack had rigged so she could see out and still reach the pedals, and left a dust trail over their driveway without even saying goodbye. Millard Mack paced the floor, his slender shoulders hunched the way tall people's shoulders often hunch. He felt guilty for not going and angry that she went without him. He paced some more, and as the guilt grew stronger than the anger, he cursed to himself, grabbed the keys to his twelve-year-old Ford pickup, and left his own dust cloud over their driveway.

That decision led directly to Millard Mack's becoming crippled.

Teensy was hard to spot in a crowd, so Millard Mack wound his way through the mass of Phlattslanders, keeping his head down to avoid eye contact and to spot Teensy's diminutive form. Eventually, he found her sitting in a chair next to a wading pool surrounded by sand. She watched small children cavort there, a large grin beaming from her face. Millard Mack stood behind her and looked down at the top of her head.

"I came," he announced.

"Good," Teensy said, but she didn't look up at him. "Pull up a chair."

"Believe I'll sit over yonder." He nodded toward the picnic tables, not yet attracting much use and, thus, the most isolated place Millard Mack could occupy. He preferred isolation.

Teensy shrugged but said nothing. Millard scanned the people milling about until his gaze reached Deedee Martin, a nineteen-year-old girl from San Angelo who had been hired to help out at BIG's Little

Store's Grand Opening Extravaganza and who owned the largest pair of breasts anyone in Phlattsland—or maybe the entire county—had ever seen, and who had been paid extra to dress in a particular fashion that day.

She wore short, crotch-hugging blue jean cut-offs and a white bikini top that barely contained the boulders on her chest. She stood by a makeshift volleyball court slathering suntan lotion on her shoulders, arms, belly, and legs. Millard Mack gasped. Millard Mack had never been particularly motivated by his libido, nor did Deedee Martin's sexualized attire stir any lustful desire in his groin. In fact, quite the opposite, what it stirred was familial nostalgia. Despite the astronomical distance between the heights and weights of Delia Mack and Deedee Martin, the latter's massive mammary glands stood out as a near-perfect match of the former's. As she bent over to lotion her legs, Millard Mack's heart ached from the absence of his mother, but his brain celebrated warm memories of her. To be clear, he had never seen his mother's breasts revealed in all their fleshiness except, perhaps, as an infant when her breasts simply meant breakfast, lunch, and dinner to him.

So the memories included all the difficult times of his young childhood, such as the deaths of his brothers, the harsh words of his father, the scraped knees, bumped heads, cuts, and bruises, when Delia Mack would pull him onto her massive lap, press him to her equally massive chest, and speak soft words or sing gentle songs to him. They included later times when Delia Mack would invite him to help knead bread dough or frost a cake or stir pots of stew, and she would visit with him about the big world outside their lives that she wanted to see: national parks, oceans, towering mountains, pine trees, and, most especially,

circuses. And they included even later times when the two of them would sit late into the evening while his father slept and they played double solitaire and planned trips to national parks, oceans, and, most especially, circuses.

"Millard Mack!" A shrill, angry voice shattered his reveries, and he became suddenly aware that Teensy stood in front of him and pounded his knees with tiny fists.

"Teensy?"

"We're going home, right now!"

"What happened?"

"You, that's what happened! You staring at that disgusting girl with the big titties."

"Aw, no, Teensy, it's not—"

"Home! Now!" She turned and marched toward the parking lot.

With Teensy's back turned, he chanced one more look at Deedee and the pleasant reminder of his mother, and then he stood and ambled to his truck, in which he would drive, he felt certain, to a most unpleasant experience with Teensy. He was right.

At home, he eased open the squeaky screen door and let it slam behind him. He went no farther into the room because Teensy sat in a raggedy easy chair with his dad's old twenty gauge shotgun lying across her lap. "Teensy," he said, more dumbfounded than afraid.

She struggled to lift the gun to her shoulder, but it was too heavy for her, so she rested it against her chest instead.

"Not that way," he said.

Her arms were too short for her to reach the trigger, so she angled it and slipped the butt under her armpit as far as necessary to get a finger inside the trigger guard.

"You'll hurt yourself. Don't," he warned. She jerked the trigger. The recoil propelled the butt backwards and the barrel up and back so that it slammed into her face. Millard Mack collapsed in a heap by the screen door, through which two pellets had ripped small holes. He groaned. He clutched his knee and groaned again. In fact, he groaned for some time. When the shock began to wane and he could focus on something other than pain, he squinted across the room toward Teensy. She sat slumped and limp in the chair, blood from her nose and mouth dripping onto her blouse and the chair. The shotgun lay at the foot of the chair.

"Teensy!" Millard Mack yelled. "Teensy!" He gritted his teeth and tried to stand, but his bloody knee refused to support him. He stretched his arms as far out in front of him as possible and slowly, awkwardly, pulled himself forward. "Teensy!"

Teensy moaned and rolled her head to the side. Her eyes struggled to open, and when they finally did open they lit upon Millard Mack sprawled on the floor, a blood smear like a snail's slime following behind him. "Millard Mack!" she yelped and propelled herself out of the chair. She stumbled to him, plopped onto the floor, and cradled his head in her lap. Tears mixed with the blood dripped from her face. "I'm sorry, Millard Mack. I'm so, so sorry."

"You're hurt," he said and reached a palm toward her cheek

"You're hurt worse. We have to get you to a doctor."

"No!"

"Don't you tell me no, Millard Mack."

"No," he said again, more gruffly than the first time. "Doctors ask questions. You'd get in terrible trouble."

"I don't care." Teensy still spoke through tears. "Your knee needs seeing to."

"Listen here," Millard Mack said in the sternest voice he had ever used with her. "My knee'll be fine, it'll heal, and I don't want you in no trouble."

Teensy grasped his face between her small palms and cried harder. "You're such a good man, Millard Mack. I promise, I won't ever shoot you again."

One way and another the two of them managed, with determination, ingenuity, and considerable awkwardness, to get Millard Mack into bed. With Teensy's constant nursing, his knee did, indeed, eventually heal, as did her smashed lips and nose, but neither healed perfectly. Her nose bent to the left for the rest of her life, and his knee would not bend at all.

And so it was that Millard Mack became crippled.

5. Elemental

Things Water Whispers to Limestone

Things Water Whispers to Limestone

Andrew Geyer

You were the only one who wanted to be the river.

Of that motley crew of brothers and sisters and first cousins you grew up among, three boys and three girls, one wanted to be an astronaut, one a composer, one a fashion model. Two weren't sure.

You? The Frio River.

Seriously. You didn't just want to float on the river, or swim in the river, or smash feetfirst into the river from a boulder or a rope swing. You didn't just want to haul bass and sunfish and catfish out of its clear and chilly depths. You wanted to *be* the river.

Why?

Reason number one was growing up on a working cattle ranch in Frio County—a ranch that the Frio River does not flow through. The only surface liquid for miles filled the 35-foot circular trough in the water lot (courtesy of the electric irrigation motor) or the smaller water troughs located at the bases of various windmills scattered across the brush and cactus-covered acreage of the Jasmine spread. Anyone who has ever tried to swim in a 35-foot circular cattle trough should appreciate why a Southwest Texas ranch boy wanted to become one with the Frio River; anyone who hasn't should take a look inside the mouth of a cow.

Need a second reason? Think Southwest Texas. Mesquite. Scrub brush. Prickly pear. The low rolling hills bristled with chaparral as far as the eye could see from the high home hill that your parents' ranch house sat atop there in your arid corner of the Chihuahuan Desert. Here's a challenge: try *not* wanting to be the Frio River next time you make the dusty drive from San Antonio south down I-35 to Hwy 57 and then west-southwest over to the Kickapoo Lucky Casino in Eagle Pass.

Number three? During a typical year in Frio County, of the ninety-two days spanning the months of June, July, and August, around seventy have high temperatures of 100 degrees Fahrenheit or above—and about 99.9% of the ranch work you grew up doing was done outside. Anyone who has ever burned prickly pear in the middle of a summer drought, with hungry cattle crowding around to gobble up the newly dethorned cacti the minute the spines are ash, has absolutely wanted to be the Frio River —whether or not they realized it at the time.

Now that the why of it has been established, focus on becoming one with the magical ribbon of 68-degree water that stretches twelve miles through the Frio River Valley from the FM 1050 bridge just above Garner State Park down to Neal's Crossing at Concan. Visualize floating at the base of the towering cliffs of Old Baldy in the clear river water with its sudden jets of cold from subterranean springs. Daydream about the majestic Bald Cypress trees lining both banks, festooned with dangling rope swings ready to fling wannabe Tarzans into the wide warmer pools and swimming holes that get colder and darker the deeper you dive. Be mindful, though, of the limestone bed that can change without warning from slippery-smooth to jagged; of the sudden rapids; of the hydraulics that lurk below the low-head dams and crossings.

The first week of June, after school let out, your Nana would always spring all six Jasmine kids—born within four years of each other, the progeny of a pair of brothers (her only sons)—from the dry and dusty heat of your daily lives and haul you up to Concan where her lifelong best friend had a house on the Frio. While the kids were becoming one with the river (well, while one of you was doing your best to, anyway), your grandmother and her bestie and their cronies stayed at the house—sometimes at the domino table on the screened porch overlooking the river and sometimes on the riverbank with cane poles—and played forty-two or hauled fish from the clear water while they drank and smoked and told tales. When you were little, even though you each had your own inner tube, the grown-ups made the smallest of you wear life jackets. Nana's best friend's husband had an old Ford truck, a faded pea green stepside with a wooden bed, and he would stuff all of you into the back with your tubes and haul you up to the FM 1050 bridge, strap a neon orange life vest onto each squealing victim, and then release you into the river. He would always wait until the last of you disappeared around the bend at the foot of Old Baldy. Then he'd head back to the doings at the river house, and you'd shuck your life vests and float through Garner State Park together, and on down.

This was long before every suburbanite in Austin and Houston and DFW had discovered that magical twelve-mile ribbon of the Frio, and converged. So once you got through Garner, particularly if it was a weekday, you'd have long stretches of river pretty much to yourselves.

Remember floating that first three miles through Garner, dodging the paddle-boats and the swimmers, then clearing the low-head dam at the foot of the park and trying not to be the first to flip? Remember scooting over the Old Leakey Road at Mager's Crossing (still trying not to flip), then scooting over the River Road at Seven Bluff Crossing (and feeling pretty good if you still hadn't flipped), and then clearing another low-head dam and shooting through the little rapid below it? Remember floating on down into The Chute where the limestone banks closed in tight and a series of standing waves always made at least some of you flip? Remember recovering your tube (it seems like you were almost always the first one who flipped) and heading on down to the gleeful madness of Comanche Crossing, and after a lazy half-mile, shooting under the bridge at Kenneth Arthur Crossing, then winding on down through the boulder garden rapid and into the three-and-a-half-foot drop at The Falls (where you nearly always flipped, all of you, especially if you didn't stay to the right)? Remember finally taking out on the beach at Neal's, even though you had your own tubes, and then enjoying the best swimming hole in the state of Texas until that old pea green Ford came and hauled you back to the river house?

You had the time of your life.

As the years passed, the smallest of you finally got to leave your life vests behind. At long last, when you were teenagers, some of you even left behind your inner tubes. In their place, you brought along snorkeling gear and floated and swam through the clear river water down to Concan. Of course, you still enjoyed the boulder diving and the rope swings and the swimming hole at Neal's. But those last couple of goggles-and-fins trips down the river were the closest you ever came to becoming one with the Frio. The whisper of water over rocks is almost comprehensible to the submerged ear. You always thought that maybe, if you could just translate a couple of syllables, you could learn the river's language—that you could come to know the things water whispers to limestone.

As the years passed, though, the river got more and more crowded. The boulders didn't tower quite as high, the rope swings didn't fling you quite as fast or far, and the swimming holes didn't seem quite as deep. Divorce came for your uncle's family, and your rambunctious band of brothers and sisters and first cousins was divided across the Lone Star State.

And of course, as you grew through adolescence and into adulthood, your wannabes changed into realities. The six of you scattered across the country. One is now a partner at a tech firm in DFW, by way of the Air Force. One is a homemaker in San Antonio. One is in the penitentiary in Wisconsin. Two are in trailer parks. One is a university professor turned department chair in South Carolina.

You don't see each other anymore, and you don't talk much even on Facebook. But you think of them often, particularly when you're in your beat-up old green canoe paddling your way down yet another ribbon of river. You still listen just as intensely to the whisper of water over limestone rocks, and you're still hoping to figure out those first two key syllables. But sometimes, especially when you're camped below a little rapid and the Milky Way is splashing starlight into the river, you take a break from listening—and wonder whether any of those other five still remember the magic of your time together during the first week of every June.

When you die, you will be cremated. Your wife, Sara, has promised to scatter your ashes in the three or four places that have the greatest significance to you. One of those places is the twelve-mile stretch of heaven that so occupied the thoughts and dreams of a Southwest Texas ranch boy. So the day will come when you finally do achieve your original wannabe, and become one with the Frio.

In the meantime, you will remember. You will remember the river.

The Goddess of the Wind and the Ghost of War

The Goddess of the Wind and the Ghost of War

Jerry Craven

Should an artist's magic graphic stone
etched with bone in hot desire
or a berry-painted frozen slate
or a canvas artwork translate
a moveless dance, a star unknown,
I'd pause and hope to learn again
the mystic truth of ice and fire:
that far and near are brethren,
that short and tall meet end to end,
that light and darkness always blend.

North of our four-spiraled Milky Way
and golden in shedding light, a gibbous moon
slides west of war perpetual on the face
of Doro-ashi, footless in a wild Lagoon
nebula tamed into the still-aired
dance of Feng-Po, goddess of snow and wind.

A crab Nebula claws toward the warrior.

Two women move without moving where stars
surround the goddess of wind; one is said
the best of ancient writers, Lady Murasaki,
the white and black of her elegance ringing,
and her tiny red-lipt face singing
with her body young in fine kimono red.
She unfolds an ancient folding fan, with grace
refuses the Doro-ashi desire for wars,
dances to unheard music's silent hum
above water green and soft stone cliffs
made for light, for waterfalls by a dancing god.
Cassini Saturn spins where mountains send
from snow bright water stilled in falling
near the gown and hidden feet of the goddess.
Beside Feng-Po and ignoring the god of wars
might be Lady Sarashina holding

a child or god or doll to join the dance
as she exposes one tiny, soft foot
searching for the stone edge of the cliff.

Three times taller than the lady in red
dances the goddess of rain and wind,
standing on a stage volcano folded into cliffs,
her hair black, her scarf (orange and gold)
drapes from her neck toward the stage
of water, her blue-clad elbows out
in dance, in peace snubs the ghost of wars,
her head held high among multi-colored stars.

On the ground, she felt slightly less powerful but no less dangerous, and she sometimes appeased herself by exerting power over men.

Terry Dalrymple

Four Visions of Virginia

Four Visions of Virginia

Terry Dalrymple

Virginia felt most alive and most in control performing stunts in her Pitts S-1T. Her favorite stunt was the vertical dive, common enough for biplane performers, but none maneuvered as daringly as she. She first headed straight up until the plane's power diminished so much that it seemed to pause in place, and then she'd reverse direction and plummet toward the ground below. She sped closer to earth, to potential death, than any other pilot had ever attempted, and she would laugh out loud, thrilled by the roar of the engine, by the speed, by the danger, and by her sense of complete self-possession. When performing for a crowd, she especially reveled in knowing that when she passed the point at which they expected her to pull up they began to wring their hands, gasp, perhaps scream. Some turned to run farther away from the site where they were sure she'd crash and burn. She did not perform the maneuver to please the crowd. She performed to terrify them, another way of building the surge of complete power she felt.

On the ground, she felt slightly less power-ful but no less dangerous, and she sometimes appeased herself by exerting power over men. Men often ogled, eyes wandering over her attractive curves and, eventually, the natural beauty of her face and her head of thick red hair. Those who stared the longest she might encourage with a smile that might have been a smirk, and her eyes would seem to say come hither and beware all at once. Those who took her up on the implied, potentially dangerous invitation, never spoke of it afterward. If someone happened to ask, they would grow pale and remain silent.

* * *

The other Virginia often performed to please. She expertly moved through her stunts, everything technically exact. When she spun into a double roll, she grinned, knowing that those below ooohed and aaahed and clapped enthusiastically. Upon landing, she eased the plane as close to the audience as possible, clambered out, and invited everyone to touch the plane and to ask questions. People shook her hand, complimented her skills, and she would look down and quietly say, "Thank you, but I'm sure you all have your own special skills." She wanted to please.

In social gatherings, she could be extremely kind, sensitive to others, demure. Men and women both appreciated her classic-ally lovely face and silky red hair. If a man asked her out, she would decline so softly and so kindly that the man had no recourse but to bow and retreat.

* * *

Yet another Virginia mostly loved freedom. As a child, she would run outside when a storm approached. She would stand, her arms spread, facing the powerful wind that brought the storm. Sometimes she struggled to stay in place against the gusts, but she stood firm, her red hair flying. That was freedom.

In later years she became a top-notch pilot, soaring alone and grinning into the wind.

And then she became a wing walker and often preferred performing that feat over flying. Out on a wing the wind was stronger than anything she'd known in childhood, and she felt as if she were the wind, as if everything about her earthbound life dissipated and all that remained was the sense of utter freedom.Not that her earthbound life was bad. At times, she could be a little grumpy, but she was generally a happy, pleasant, outgoing individual. She loved gatherings with friends, and she dated casually, but had found no one—and felt no hurry to do so—with whom she might develop a serious relationship. Most men caught on quickly, and the few who didn't and pushed for something steadier or more exclusive were gently rebuffed. If a man still pushed, she stood solid, facing his onslaught as she had once faced the wind. And she felt free.

* * *

Those who knew Virginia or had seen her perform or had heard or read about her came to idolize her for her aerial antics, her daring, her strength, her power, her quiet sense of self, her humility, and her freedom. Her followers became something like a cult that worshipped the flying woman with red hair. They deified her and called her Angel of the Air.

6. The Ties that Bind

There's Something About Harry

There's Something About Harry

Andrew Geyer

1. *Choir loft*

It's Sunday, and you're attending the funeral of a dear old friend at the Highland Park United Methodist Church in Florence, South Carolina. You were frankly hesitant because of the COVID pandemic, but were asked by your friend Harry's widow to speak at the service and felt like you had to go. The call, which came on your office phone, landed like a combination punch: first the sound of Liv's voice after all these years, then the fact of Harry's death and her request that you give some sort of eulogy. The service would be live-streamed, Liv said, with inperson attendance by invitation only. She assured you the event would be safely distanced and every-one would be wearing masks.

Well, guess what? Nope.

From your perch on the chair loft, here is what you see: people moving the blocking signs from the chairs they aren't supposed to sit in and sitting there anyway; people hugging, shaking hands—it's a freaking COVID bonanza.

But the virus denial isn't the worst part. Not by a long shot. The worst part is the pictures—or rather, the lack thereof. What's being pictured, that is, and what isn't. *Odd*, you think as you watch the super-spreader event unfold in super slow mo in the chapel below, doesn't come close to covering it. But while you wait with the other mourners who are scheduled to speak (all of whom have unmasked and are sitting in a pack after moving the blocking signs from their chairs), *odd* is the word you keep coming back to. You find yourself thinking of Margaret Atwood—which is odd in and of itself—and something

she wrote in *The Handmaid's Tale*: "Context is all; or is it ripeness? One or the other."

So. To begin again at the beginning; or is it the middle?

2. *Context*

That particular Sunday dawned crisp and glorious, the October sky deep blue and cloudless, the leaves finally starting to burn orange and gold and red. After a brisk five-mile loop pushing your four-year-old daughter in the running stroller, you kissed your wife Sara and said goodbye to all four of your kids and started the two-hour drive from Aiken up to Florence, by way of Columbia. You passed the time thinking about Harry—dead of a heart attack at age fifty-four, his widow-maker artery 75% blocked—and your seven years as best friends, virtually all of which had been spent in and around Columbia and during which you were inseparable. That's what you were asked to talk about at the funeral, as part of a "Witness to the Life" segment of the event. But you hadn't seen Harry in twenty-five years and had no clue what you were going to say. You'd never been one for canned speeches. As a university professor recently turned department chair, you felt comfortable speak-ing in front of an audience and planned to extemporize your comments, in part depending on what other speakers said.

But still . . .

As you drove across the Broad River that ran wide and shallow and gray-green in a rocky bed, you remembered canoeing it with Harry thirty years ago. It was your first time together in a boat. You put in at Peak and floated sixty miles of blackwater down through the heart of downtown Columbia, where the Broad and the Saluda flow together to make the Congaree, and on down through the Congaree Swamp to take out at the Highway 601 bridge. Over the course of your time as best friends, you'd canoed hundreds of miles of rivers in three states—drinking beer and eating fish you caught and camping along the banks of wild streams.

You'd come to Columbia for graduate school and Harry was there to learn the restaurant business. When you weren't playing together, you worked together at a place called Dixie Fish. Harry running the bar and you waiting tables and bartending sometimes and all the Dixie folks hanging out after the place closed and drinking beer and then going out and doing shots and drinking even more beer and playing pool. The two of you co-ruled a green felt kingdom—playing eight-ball for pitchers and table stakes against all comers. Harry was the only person you'd ever seen who actually got better at pool over the course of an evening: the more he drank, the better he shot. How many times had you seen Harry pound a pint and then run the table—leaning in over his bridge, squinting his eyes, and stroking the kill shot home with a crooked grin? And when the bars finally closed, you climbed onto your motorcycles and rode home, more often than not with the soft and supple arms of a member of the fairer sex (one of whom was Liv) rapped tightly around your waists.

3. *Ripeness*

The folks at the Dixie Fish were more like a family than just people you worked with: Harry and you and Elizabeth (who you married at the end of your and Harry's time together in Columbia, but later divorced) and Alisha and Bonnie and Brave and Tommy and Gladys and all the hangers-on and the movers-through (one of whom turned out to be Liv). You shared tips and time, drinking and smoking and sleeping together in ramshackle houses with lots of bedrooms. Living your twenties. Free and easy and in the moment. Squeezing the juice out of every day and night.

And all the while you and Harry canoed, learned to sail, took flying lessons—taking off and landing and taking off and landing in single-engine planes on grassy airfields across South Carolina. No fear. Ever. Bulletproof and immortal. Completely alive.

And now . . . what?

4. *Odd*

After pulling into the parking lot of the Highland Park United Methodist Church in Florence (your maroon Kia Sorento like an orphan stepchild at a family reunion of BMWs, Volvos, Lexus, Mercedes), after making your way past mourners standing unmasked in close groups (the women high-heeled and gorgeous; the men in Brooks Brothers suits, cap-toe Oxfords polished to a high sheen; and you in your black dress shirt and tie, black dress jeans, black Justin boots, and a gray-and-black-patterned sport coat feeling like the brother of your orphan-stepchild car), after walking into the church and finding the reception desk for the funeral service and being issued a black mask (made by your wife Sara, your own mask featured brown and black horses galloping across a field of green cloth), and then being led up to the choir loft to wait for the service to begin, you have yet to see a single familiar face. Not one.

The program you were given at the reception desk has a photo on the cover. The man in the photo is at the wheel of a big Boston

Whaler with three fat Mercury engines in tandem across the back. The caption reads: *Service of Death and Resurrection of Harold Harlan Pharr, October 4, 2020*. The man in the photo doesn't even look like Harry (who, you remember, always hated the name Harold). The man in the photo has a paunch and jowls. His legs are pale and flabby. Harry, who once climbed The Nose at El Capitan—bivying overnight on a narrow ledge halfway up the sheer rockface—was lean-muscled and tanned. This cannot, you think, be him. But as you search the face (partially hidden by dark sunglasses and a pulled-down cap), you can't help but make out that crooked kill-shot grin that so defined the Harry you knew back in your twenties.

And you don't know what to think about that.

There are video screens at intervals around the walls of the church with pictures of Harry's life flashing across them. But you register only now that the photos have been sequenced into a montage. They begin with pictures of a wiry kid sporting Harry's grin and posing in succession with baseballs, fishing rods, hunting rifles, and finally a car as he moves from boyhood through adolescence. Next comes a lean young man in a Cadet uniform from the Citadel with that same kill-shot grin. Then suddenly Harry and Liv are standing next to each other in a tuxedo and wedding gown (Liv drifted out of the Dixie Fish crowd, but reconnected with Harry later; you received a courtesy invitation but were out in Texas trying to avoid what eventually became a messy divorce from Elizabeth, and knew better than to attend). Next Harry is rubbing Liv's very pregnant belly, and in the succeeding frame he's kissing their newborn baby son. Then comes another belly-rubbing photo and another just-kissed baby son. Vacation photos follow: the family together in the mountains, on boats, in front of signature buildings in various tourist destinations as Harry and the boys age and Liv seems to remain unchanged.

You find yourself wondering what happened to the pictures from the years you and Harry spent as best friends. You remember taking such pictures: photos of Harry and yourself winning at pool, paddling canoes, climbing rockfaces, looking out the windows of single-engine planes, standing astride motorcycles with members of the fairer sex seated behind (you clearly recall Liv being in at least one of them). And what about the myriad photos of your own wedding to Elizabeth (at which Harry served as best man)? The day after the wedding, Harry left Columbia for Florence to open a Zaxby's restaurant; you headed to Texas for your first teaching job at Austin Community College. Before you went your separate ways, Harry offered you a partnership in the Zaxby's venture; but you answered that your first, best destiny was in the classroom, and your time with Harry came to a close.

Your part of Harry's life seems to have been edited out of the montage.

On a hunch, you open the program. On the inside flap is a bio of Harry that doesn't even contain the words *Dixie Fish* but goes on for paragraph after paragraph about the chain of restaurants Harry built, his excellence as a husband and father, his generous gifts to the Highland Park United Methodist Church. A detailed schedule for the service follows, complete with the names of dozens of people you don't recognize in addition to your own: *Dr. Joseph Jasmine*.

On the view screens, Harry keeps getting grayer. Paler. Flabbier. He doesn't look good. But he keeps getting nicer stuff as, beside him, his boys grow into adolescence and Liv remains unchanged. Bigger boats. Higher-end hunting and camping gear. And the destination cities of the buildings the family poses in front of keep getting more exotic. About the only thing from your twenties that you finally recognize (besides Liv) are the bottles. Harry is drinking in virtually every photo, and the bottles from the palest and flabbiest years are all top-shelf.

Harry got rich.

It hits you with the force of an epiphany. Not just a little bit rich, either. He got all the way there. According to the bio, Harry died owning dozens of Zaxby's restaurants. The opening speaker on the program, you see only now, is a Zaxby's corporate VP. What a way to become a millionaire. It certainly explains the paunch, the jowls, the flab. And of course, the heart attack: fried food and booze and the mad scramble that is the business of fast food.

Harry worked himself to death.

So. To end at the ending; or is it the middle, still?

5. *There's something about Harry*

It suddenly occurs (or rather, reoccurs) to you, as the photos fade from the viewing screens, that you and Harry are the same age. Were the same age. Whatever. Something seems to have gone all wrong with time. You take out your phone, open the camera app, study the face reflected in the cell phone screen. Your face.

But still . . .

The cheeks behind the black mask remain lean and tanned, but the eyes are lined with crow's feet and the weather-creased forehead is topped with thin gray hair. You can't help but remember that, when you were burning through your twenties back in Columbia, you sported a thick blonde ponytail. Gone. And

Harry gone. And Elizabeth gone. And all those Dixie Fish folks that were like family? In the mostly maskless crowd in the chapel below, you see not a single one.

So: context or ripeness?

What if the answer is neither one? That's the question you're facing now. Is there nothing left of those Dixie days? No legacy at all? Nothing but the gift of COVID that is being shared by the pallbearers in the front row below with their masks pulled down, and by the crowd of strangers sitting too close together behind them?

What about the face you see reflected in your own phone screen?

The family begins processing into the church and everyone in the chapel rises. You rise with them. As the video screens around the walls go dark, you stow your cell phone in your jacket pocket. The assembled mourners begin to sing "Holy, Holy, Holy," but you don't know the words. And anyway, you're focused on Liv.

She's still beautiful. A long black gown perfectly complements her thick dark hair that is still backswept, unsalted with gray, and her pale and perfect skin (still unlined somehow) and her eyes that are as dark and luminous as her darkly lustrous hair. How many nights did you stare into those eyes after a motorcycle ride home with those pale, lithe arms locked tight around your waist? Flanked by two young men who are a mix of herself and Harry, Liv does not look up to meet your choir-loft gaze.

Finally, the service starts and you follow along in the program. Mixed in among the *Words of Grace* and the *Opening Prayer* and the *Words of Welcome* (as listed on page 3) are details about Harry's impact as a member of the Methodist Church. And the *Old Testament Lesson* (Psalm 95: 1-7), the *Gospel Lesson* (1 John 3:16-18), even the solo performance of

"How Great Thou Art" and the sermon that follows are all intertwined with the story of Harry's gifts to the church and his impact on the lives of the many people who worked in his restaurants.

You recognize and respect all those legacies. But what, you keep asking yourself, about the Dixie days?

The *Witness to the Life* section begins with the Zaxby's VP, and as he extols Harry's work ethic and his profound business sense, you keep trying to nail down your own brief part in Harry's fifty-four-year journey from cradle to grave. What to say? And what about your own legacy? You keep getting distracted by what-ifs. What if you'd taken Harry up on his partnership offer? Would you and Elizabeth have avoided the awful mess that starving on two jobs in Austin, Texas helped make of your marriage? Would you and Liv have rekindled your flame instead? Would Harry still have worked himself to death?

You're scheduled to speak second. As the Zaxby's VP finishes, you get up, walk down to the podium, unmask, and take a long last look at Liv. Her dark eyes are shining with tears as they finally rise to meet yours.

You nod, pull the cell phone from your jacket pocket, open the camera app, set the phone on the podium so that your own face is reflected on the screen. Then you pull out the mask that Sara made for you and set it beside the phone. And you stand before the assembled strangers (except for Liv) looking exactly like what you are—a professor turned department chair, in your fifties, with a wife and four kids you adore, and with a mortgage and a car payment and a big chunk of student loan debt; a man who will never be rich, and who faces the very real possibility of never being able to retire—and feeling, suddenly and forever, perfectly fine with that.

You'll always have those Dixie days. Their memory is one of the main reasons you brought Sara and the kids back to South Carolina to live. And with that realization, you finally know what to say.

"As I watched the photo montage of Harry's life, I found myself thinking of a quote by Margaret Atwood: *Context is all; or is it ripeness? One or the other.*" You pause, scan the crowd, then do your best imitation of Harry's crooked kill-shot grin. "With all due respect to Margaret Atwood, Harry and I had both. *Context, ripeness*, they were the same. We shared our twenties together, you see, along with a family of fellow-travelers we met at a place called Dixie Fish. I didn't see any pictures of that time in the montage, but it doesn't matter. Pictures wouldn't do those years justice anyway. We were young and beautiful together, three sheets to the wind on life, and every breath we took was a miracle. Let me tell you our story . . ."

Lady Agnes and the Mountain Man

Lady Agnes and the Mountain Man

Jerry Craven

Agnes lounged on a hand-carved chair in the gem patio when Buster licked the contact from her left eye.

She pushed the dog aside and blinked. Buster tossed his head back and swallowed. "Did you see that?" she demanded. "Did you? Your damned effing dog ate my blue contact lens."

"Never," Fenimore said, "grow accustomed to uttering oaths."

Was that a rebuke, Agnes wondered, or just another of his annoying aphorisms? She watched his face for a clue, and she tried for a smile.

"Buster saw the lens," Fenimore said, "thought it trash. Removed it."

"By eating it? That's so creepy."

He regarded her with a steady stare that often unnerved her, put a finger on his cheek, under his left eye. "Heterochromia," he said and nodded.

She wondered if the nod was a nonverbal statement of approval or a criticism. Just in case, she gave him her best smile, for she felt pleased he used a word few people knew, and she tried not to show annoyance that he spoke a single word instead of making a complete statement. "What did you mean when you used that term? Of course I know what the word means. But what did you mean in saying it?"

"Opals."

One word. Agnes sighed. So annoying. She let her smile fade, looked back at the odd black cross of a crystal she had been inspecting when Buster licked her eye.

She tried to be irritated with Fenimore for his clipped answer, though she did understand what he meant, for he had just weeks before given her a birthday gift of two magnificent fire opals, gems she learned later, he had bought from Coober Pedy.

He had pointed at the blue stone. "Right," he said, then pointing at the green stone, he said, "Left." A compliment, Agnes realized, though she knew her eyes were far more weird than pretty. He had said he liked her eyes, compared them to his best opals.

She grudgingly admitted to herself that she understood. So more words weren't crucial— but she wanted to hear them, anyway, wanted him to say her eyes were beautiful. His obvious discomfort caused her to change the subject. "What is this funny little black stone?" She held it up. The question appeared to please him.

"From Arroyo Hondo," Fenimore said.

"Wherever it came from, it's ugly."

"First learn, and then form opinions."

Another aphorism, Agnes thought, though now, coming from Fenimore, it had become a cliché, and aimed at me it is a criticism. "Okay, Okay, okay. Then tell me what it is."

"Staurolite. Common term: fairy cross. Tiny garnets occur in the black schist."

She looked with new appreciation at the stone. "You're right. Nothing named star light can be ugly. And fairy cross is a wonderful name. Also, I like garnets, however small."

Fenimore raised his voice in spelling out the word: *staur-o-lite.*

"Oh. Not star light." Agnes felt disappointment wash over her, along with a twinge of resentment for the way he corrected her.

"We can go to my staurolite mine."

"Where is this gemstone mine of yours?"

He eyed her with his head turned and tilted, a gesture she figured was some sort of disapproval. "I told you."

"I apologize," she said. "You did tell me. Still, why didn't you simply say Arroyo Hondo again?"

"Say little, do much."

Agnes stared. Was he now coaching himself in such maddening brevity by using his own cliches? "It would be a good hike for the two of us," she said. "How about we go in the cool of the morning?"

"Tomorrow." He punctuated the word with a curt nod, a dismissal of the subject, Agnes thought, and of me.

"It's so clear to me that I annoy you with my many questions and my insistence on talking. I'll be the first to admit that I talk too much, for it has been my lifelong habit to overtalk everything. You undertalk, did you know that? You speak in tidy little packages of words or else word. I want more, much more, and you want less from me." She paused, waited, and finally asked, "Have you no comment about what I said?"

"There is a time to keep silent and a time to speak."

Agnes threw up her hands.

During the night she spent some time asking herself why she chose to live with Fenimore.

They had first seen each other on the last leg of her flight from Amarillo to Taos, and she took the seat beside him because he had a rugged and almost ugly masculine look to him that she liked. He answered her many questions with short statements or single words, and when she discovered he liked gemstones, she asked many questions. He had something intelligent to say about each stone she mentioned, and his extensive knowledge of gems made him even more attractive.

When she commented with admiration about how succinct and to the point his statements were, he explained that his mother had given him a book of aphorisms, and that he still had the book, still read and reread it, and worked to follow its advice. "It praises brevity," he said. At the time, she admired Fenimore for what she saw as a dedication to wisdom.

He invited her to his house on the desert south of Taos, and once there she saw that he had built the house, decorated it with displays of gemstones, had made the furniture, even the chair in his gem-laden patio, her favorite place to lounge.

On their hike in Arroyo Hondo, she asked him to sit beside her on an outcropping of rock. Buster walked around them, impatient, Agnes thought, and annoyed that they stopped walking. He tugged on Fenimore's cuff, then gave up and went on down. "Now is as good a time as any," Agnes said, "for us to talk about us. Are you okay with that?"

He responded with his level gaze, then spoke a clipped single word. "Talk."

"We both will talk. I have some important questions, and don't respond with one of your impressive clichés or aphorisms or whatever you call those small bits of words that sound so wise but are not. Answer my questions even if they sound silly to you. We both know how irritating I can be, and crabby, yet you seem to want me to stay with you. Why? And don't you dare answer with only one word or with a bundle of slick words written hundreds of years ago for people to memorize and cough up as a fake replacement for real feeling."

Agnes thought Fenimore looked astounded, but she wasn't sure, for she had never before seen or heard anything from him that was close to astonishment. "You're leaving me?" he asked.

"Three words. That's movement in the

right direction. My answer to that is I don't know, though I will say you need to talk some more. Right now."

"Don't leave."

"Don't you dare fall back to only two words. Give me some reason to stay. Tell me how you feel about me."

"You're beautiful."

"Not good enough. I know I'm beautiful, even if one of my eyes is the wrong color."

"Be patient, please. Such talking is new, difficult. The ancient ones always knew that the soul stamps itself upon the body. Morality and beauty are essentially the same."

She lifted a finger in warning. "No clichés or aphorisms," she cautioned.

"Your green eye is perfect in its beauty, as is the blue . . ."

"My eyes are not the same size, and that's hardly a thing of beauty."

". . . and both sing of the beauty of your soul. Your beauty is pure because you are moral and good to your very core." He fell silent and looked at her with what she hoped was genuine tenderness.

"So? Tell me what you make of what you see as good in me. What does it mean to you?"

"That is the reason, the reason . . ."

"That's six words. Good. But you'd better finish the sentence."

". . . that I. That I. You know. The reason that I. Care. Yeah. That I care. About you."

Agnes stood and leaned into him in a sudden, quick motion, and she kissed his forehead. "You can stop talking for a while, but you need to memorize how you did it without all those pre-cooked words. Right now, take me to your mine and help me find some star light."

Twice before, I had failed her in the hospitality department, so this time I leaned over and accepted her embrace.

Terry Dalrymple

City Courtship

City Courtship

Terry Dalrymple

I hate to admit this, but my fortieth birthday made me a little crazy. It reminded me that I'd been divorced twice before turning thirty and hadn't had a decent relationship since. The P.I. business is hell on relationships. I'll say it, I was lonely. So I moved to a little suburb west of the city, sure that I could find work and meet a nice gal to spend time with, maybe even marry. But at forty-two I was still single, with few friends, and I was bored. And lonely.

That's why when Brady O'Brien called and said he really needed me rightaway, I didn't hesitate. The aggrieved wife who'd hired me to gather proof of her philandering husband's unfaithfulness could wait. Those cases were a good chunk of my bread and butter, but I hated them. They were always ugly and depressing. I figured working in the city again might provide some excitement.

As police commissioner, Brady mostly sat behind a desk; but in his earlier days on the force, he'd been known as the best cop in Houston. He stood only five-seven and had a slender, wiry frame. Still, he'd always had a reputation as "that feisty little guy" who could take down men three times his size. But when I arrived he was at the desk looking worn and tired. His office was, as usual, nearly bare. Other than his plain desk and chair, and a chair for visitors, there was no other furniture. In his job, he could probably have whatever he wanted in there at the city's expense, but he preferred simple, plain. A minimalist. The walls, too, were bare, except for a framed photo of his family from a few years back and another of him grinning and standing next to a huge, hanging marlin he'd caught twenty years

before.

He was also a no-nonsense, get-to-the-point guy. After a couple brief pleasantries, he filled me in. Someone was playing pipes, the instrument, so loud every night that they could be heard for several miles. No one in my little burb had heard the music, but I'd read all about it in the papers, which called the pipes *Pan's flute*. The playing had been heard for ten nights in a row, always starting at dark and lasting until midnight. It affected everyone, but especially younger folks—teens, twenty-somethings.

"They go crazy," Brady said, "swarming outside, chanting jibberish, dancing in the streets, hugging and kissing and who knows what other kinds of debauchery."

I worked hard to repress a smile, thinking how I wouldn't at all mind a little debauchery myself. Brady didn't notice, just kept talking.

He had formed a special force to track the perpetrator down, but they had failed completely. And then a boy went missing. And then a second. I found a stubby pencil and a receipt in my jacket pocket and wrote their names down on the back of the receipt.

When I arose to leave, Brady said, "One more thing. That music, it makes me a little crazy, too. Makes me feel weird, feelings I'm not used to."

"Like what?"

"Never mind. I'm just saying gird your loins when the music starts."

I grinned briefly. I mean seriously, does anybody really say that? "Okay," I said, "they'll be girded."

That night I found a hotel not far from a heavily populated residential neighborhood.

When the pipes started, I walked outside and headed toward that neighborhood. I could see what Brady O'Brien was talking about. The music lifted my spirits, sent a tingle through me I hadn't felt in many years, a feeling that urged me get a little crazy, dance in the street, kiss a woman, any woman. Which reminded me how lonely I'd been. I guess I forgot to gird up. But having trained myself to stifle emotion on a case, I let it all go.

In the neighborhood, young folks filled the streets, the sidewalks, the yards. They chanted garble I couldn't make sense of, danced, held hands, hugged, kissed, stretched out in yards and did more than kiss. I watched for a bit, studying individuals as best I could, then chose a girl maybe eighteen or nineteen. She some-how appeared to know better than most what she was doing, why she was there. I very lightly curled my hand around her wrist, and when she turned I released and raised my hands in the air.

"No harm," I said. "Just a question or two."

She gave me a once-over look, then another, and then a third. She was tall, leggy, and lovely, and when she cocked her head her long dark hair fell across her face in a tantaliz-ing way. But I do have morals. I never go after young girls. She finally nodded. "Okay, Mr. Curious, ask your questions."

We talked for thirty minutes or so. I had picked right. She was a goldmine, even knew one of the boys who disappeared and said he had returned but was staying with someone named Kay. Kay was twenty-two and had her own apartment. He stayed with her because he didn't want his parents or the police to know he was back. I asked where he had been. "Who knows," she said. "He hasn't even told Kay, much less me. He seems embarrassed about it."

"Where's this apartment?"

She pointed. "End of the block, turn left. A couple blocks from there you'll see the com-plex."

I got the apartment number from her and headed that way.

When the boy answered the door, I stepped in without invitation and closed the door behind me. He turned away, strolled to the kitchen, and pulled a beer from the fridge.

"Who are you?" he asked with his back turned. "And do you want a beer?"

I told him my name and accepted the beer. We sat in what passed for a living room. Posters of musicians hung on the walls by thumbtacks. A cd player sat on one shelf with stacks of cds beside it, maybe two hundred or so. Higher shelves contained books, mostly self-help stuff and some about women's empowerment, cultural revolution, Zen, Buddhism, and a couple that looked new about paganism.

I played it straight, told him what I wanted and why. Told him I meant no harm and would not reveal his whereabouts. We had three beers before he opened up. The pipe player had abducted him but let him go shortly afterwards. He remembered the street he'd been on when she nabbed him. That was the first time I knew the perp was a woman. He did not know how she amplified the sound so that the whole city could hear. He refused to explain why she'd released him. On the back of my receipt I wrote his description of the area where she'd gotten him. It was only about eight blocks from where I was. I started pounding the pavement.

As I moved nearer the area, the music's volume never altered, never louder, never quieter. How did she do that? I found the street the boy had named, a street that appeared to be in a commercial district with stores and shops lining the sidewalks. No restaurants, no bars, and at that hour—ten—all the establishments were closed and, I assumed, locked up tight. I stuck close to the storefronts and walked slow and quiet, my eyes darting from down to across the street. Nothing. I walked straight for another block. Nothing. I turned onto an intersecting street and covered the block. Nothing. But as I stepped off the curb at the crosswalk, my peripheral vision caught just a glimpse of movement about half a block down to my right.

If it were her, she had likely seen me, too, so I dispensed with the slow, quiet walk and ran as hard as I could in that direction. I thought I saw a shadow-like figure move into deeper darkness, and as I approached that spot I could tell that the deeper darkness was an alley. I skidded around the corner into the alley. Rookie mistake. Her foot caught me straight in the groin, and I went down hard, gasping for breath. My head spun from hitting the pavement, but I could think clearly enough to know that this was not the kind of excitement I had hoped a trip to the city would provide.

I had just begun to catch my breath and stop gritting my teeth when the woman reached a hand down to help me up. I took the offered hand, surprised at how soft and warm it felt. I guess I expected something more like a devil's clawed hand. I grunted as she helped pull me to my feet, and when I was far enough up to balance, I released my grip and swung for her nose. Bad form, I know, swinging at a woman. She dodged the blow, then grabbed the lapels of my jacket and jerked me toward her until our faces were maybe one inch apart. Her breath was warm and smelled sweet, nothing like a devil's breath, I assume. . .

"What the hell?" she said. "I helped you up and you try to punch me?"

"You kicked me in the nuts."

"And you should never hit a woman."

"But you kicked me in the nuts."

She released me. "Okay, okay, I did kick you in the nuts. Good point. But you encroached on my territory."

"It's a public sidewalk. And alley."

"Who the hell are you?"

We both seemed to have calmed a bit. I took a deep breath and released it. "Eddie," I said. "Eddie Blaze. I'm a P.I. Who the hell are you?"

"Pandora. Just Pandora. I'm a flute player."

I asked her if we could step out of the alley where the street lights would give us a better view of each other. She moved that way. I followed. In the light I first noticed that she was beautiful. Or maybe cute's a better word. I'm never sure. She had creamy white skin and only a few wrinkles, crow's feet, I guess, at the corners of her eyes. Her lips were full and pink, the color, I assumed, created with lipstick, but I later discovered differently, discovered her lips really were that color. She sported what I think would be called a sassy short haircut, the hair light brown and silky. Her clothing consisted only of a long white gown that could well have been a robe or a toga.

I looked back at her face. "So, Pandora, huh?"

"Yes, Pandora."

I chuckled. Just a little. "Have you opened your box?"

She grinned coyly. Or so it seemed to me. "A number of times."

"I guess that's why all those evils are out in the world."

"Oh, no. My box contains only sweetness,

tenderness, joy."

I lost myself for a moment imagining what her body looked like under that robe. I chuckled again. "I'll bet." Then I got hold of myself and said, "You've been hard to find."

She shrugged. "You found me."

"My lucky night."

"Could be."

I straightened my spine, cleared my throat. "Why'd you kidnap those boys?"

She scoffed. "I didn't kidnap them. Just invited them to join me for a while."

"I found one, but he's not talking. Where's the other?"

"Beats me."

Apparently, she wasn't going to explain much, so I tried a different subject. "How do you make that flute audible all over the city?"

"There's much I can do that you wouldn't understand."

"A sorceress, are you?

"Something like that."

Unsure of what she meant, I stuck to the main subject. "You've made a lot of people mad in this city what with that music making the kids go wild."

A stray dog barked down the street. Another answered from farther off.

"The kids aren't mad. Anyway, the music makes everyone go wild. The adults just can't accept that kind of joy."

The closer dog loped off in the direction of the farther.

"I'll admit, I felt it and fought it, but I did enjoy it." She smiled and nodded. It was a pretty smile. I had an idea. "Did you want to enjoy it yourself? Is that why you took those boys?"

She seemed miffed that I had asked. "Okay, sure, why wouldn't I want to? But I should know better. I'm a woman. Boys just aren't satisfying."

I took a chance and very gently placed my hand on her shoulder. She flinched but then relaxed and let my hand remain. "I'm not a boy." I thought maybe I was overstepping but, to be honest, I had become overwhelmed with the thought of spending some time with her. Hell, right then I'd have married her if she wanted.

She looked hard at my face, then smiled, hunched the shoulder on which my hand lay, bent her neck, and pressed her cheek against my knuckles. After a moment, she dropped her shoulder but kept smiling. I said, "How do you feel about suburbs?"

"I guess they're okay."

"Mine's a little burb west of here. Maybe you could visit."

"Maybe."

That seemed encouraging. "Or maybe you could come stay for a while."

The coy look again, then, "Maybe."

"If you do," I said, "you'll have to quit playing those pipes." Her face fell and she shrugged my hand off her shoulder. "I mean loud. You'll have to quit playing so loud, however you do that. But you can play for me all you want. For you and me, no one else. How would that be?"

She looked away from me and remained silent for a full thirty seconds or so. Finally, she turned and said quietly, "Might be okay."

I'm not exactly a smooth operator and, weak as it might have been, my approach up to that point was all I had. I couldn't do any better, so I said the only thing I could think of. "That's two maybes and a might. So I'm going to walk away. I'm going to walk to my car, and I'm going to drive back here in about fifteen minutes. If you bolt, I won't come after you again and I won't tell anyone I found you. But if you stay, maybe hide in the alley, we'll drive away tonight, straight to that little suburb. Okay?"

She smiled, but I didn't know whether it was because she could get away or because she would wait. "Okay," she said.

I walked to the corner, but as soon as I was out of her sight I broke into a lope. All the way back to my car, I thought about the loneliness I'd been feeling for so long, thought about how Pandora could relieve that loneliness, thought I was crazy for asking a woman I didn't know to live with me, thought I'd be crazy if I didn't ask. But most of all, I hoped that she'd be there when I arrived, that she'd smile and, her flowing white gown shining in the dome light, that she would slide into the seat beside me. And I'd have solved another crime. Maybe two.

And finally I wrote a poem, though the
words in it seemed to spin wildly around,
knocking together within the lines,
clanging between them.
Jerry Craven

7. Love Light

What Ever Happened to the Girl with the Wishing Flower?

What Ever Happened to the Girl with the Wishing Flower?

Andrew Geyer

1. Specter—Aiken, SC

It's February 5th, 2021 and you're drifting, staring out the window at the drizzle that continues to fall as another gray day fades into evening. Your 4-year-old daughter-by-blood snuggles against you on the couch, your 18-year-old stepdaughter (who you've raised since age six as your daughter-by-blood) sits across the living room in front of the bank of windows that overlooks the lake, the two of them watching *Entertainment Tonight*. You vaguely register, reflected in the glass, flashing porcelain veneers and slick production. It's been another grueling day in an academic year the COVID has stretched into a decade, and the only things left on your radar are the last bit of daylight gently rippling on the surface of the water, the takeout on its way home with your wife and sons, and early bed.

Until you see the ghost of Vicki Lynn Hogan appear in the window—and you are suddenly, absolutely, wide-awake.

It's not the first time you've seen her—the square jaw, the high cheekbones, the eyes that seem to stare through you into someplace else—but it's been a while, and the glob of ice in your belly feels more like sick dread than fear. The long-dead face you see, the face of a 12-year-old the rest of the world later came to know as Anna Nicole Smith, is like a wormhole sucking you back into the past.

You met her on the Frio River in Texas. Vicki Lynn was the grandniece of the woman who owned the river house your Nana brought you to every June. Two years younger, but a decade older in worldliness, she smelled like the river. She asked you to pluck her a flower, as you floated downstream together, from a bank of glorious dandelions. But as you reached for a bright yellow blossom, she said, "No, a wishing flower." And you understood, plucking instead a delicate globe of feathery seeds that her breath sent wafting into the water. When you asked what she'd wished for, she said, "If I tell you, it might not come true."

Later, on a riverbank lit by fireflies, she kissed you. The crescent moon seemed to float on the surface of the water, and the two of you were half-arguing, but mostly flirting, about whether the name of the town she was being sent to live in with her mother's sister was pronounced MEKseea (her) or MehEEa (you)—it's name was, and is, Mexia—and you were right, but it was Texas. Then suddenly, her lips were pressing against yours. As were other parts of her, all moving against you in ways you'd only dreamed of. But you were too much of a kid, and too intimidated, to do more than just kiss; until finally she pulled back, sighed, whispered in your ear, "I wished to become Anna Nicole." Then she was gone, leaving you and the fireflies to wonder what the hell she meant by that.

Back in the present moment of your South Carolina living room, with Beatrice and Ariel and *Entertainment Tonight*, you find yourself wondering yet again where 12-year-old Vicki Lynn learned so much about things carnal. You ask yourself for the hundredth time whether, if you'd come to that realization on the bank of the Frio—and found the guts to say something about it later at the river house—the slow-motion train wreck of that wish-come-true could somehow have been avoided.

Then the dead girl's voice whispers inside your head that the ghost isn't outside the window, but on TV.

You snap your head around and find yourself staring into the face of Dannielynn Birkhead, the late Anna Nicole Smith's now-teenaged daughter. *Entertainment Tonight* is previewing a *20/20* episode set to air later this evening in which Dannielynn travels with her father to her mother's hometown. And Dannielynn Birkhead looks exactly the same as that 12-year-old who kissed you on the river.

Your head tries to tell you that a reflection is all you've seen. But the better part of you knows that the specter of Vicki Lynn Hogan is every bit as real as your daughter-by-blood beside you and your stepdaughter across the room.

2. *Bum steer—Columbia, SC*

It's January 29th, 1996 and you're a bit confused as you pull this month's issue of *Texas Monthly* from the latest cardboard care package your mother mailed from Frio County, Texas to Columbia, South Carolina. On the cover is a photo of Anna Nicole Smith in a bright red dress, superimposed over the words *BUM STEER AWARDS*.

Having grown up on a working cattle ranch in Southwest Texas—the place where the cowboy was born—you can't remember a time when you didn't know the meaning of the term *bum steer*. So *Texas Monthly's* announcement that the 1996 Bum Steer of the Year is Anna Nicole Smith leaves you scratching your head.

Bum Steer? Anna Nicole Smith? Hmm . . . That's not how you remember her. If anything, it was you who were the bum steer that night on the Frio with the girl who wished to become Anna Nicole.

To your admittedly testosterone-driven imagination, there is nothing bum about Anna Nicole Smith—unless of course they're referring to *her bum* (something you've thought about often since *Playboy* revealed its buxom glory in 1992 and again in 1993). And *steer*? Steers and the 1993 Playmate of the Year lie about as far apart on your reality spectrum as violet and red on the color spectrum.

But the main reason you can't wrap your head around that Bum Steer of the Year Award is that you and Anna Nicole are almost the same age. You chalk up to the foibles of youth her libidinous escapades: the infamous "wardrobe malfunction" at the Planet Hollywood opening, the "White Trash Nation" issue of *New York* magazine, her marriage to octogenarian J. Howard Marshall, and even the debacle of his dueling funerals a year later. You have, after all, some foibles of your own (although the scope of your indiscretions is decidedly less epic). Besides, you're both pursuing your dreams—she with her modeling career and first modestly successful bit parts in films, you with a PhD in Comparative Literature and first scholarly publications.

Why can't *Texas Monthly*, you ask yourself, cut Anna Nicole Smith some slack?

But in the same way that ANS fades from the silver screen after the *To the Limit* box office bomb, her life antics—libidinous and otherwise—fade from your conscious thoughts. Between adjuncting a jillion classes, fruitlessly searching for a full-time job in academe without a published book, a marriage of your own, and the birth of a son, you catch glimpses of ANS occasionally over the next few years—CNN updates about her long and ugly spousal support lawsuit against the Marshall estate, features on *Entertainment Tonight* about this new love interest or that new public binge.

But like that night on the river after you lost your nerve, there is no further connection between the two of you.

3. *Spectacle—Austin, TX*

Then in 2001, with her starring role in *The Anna Nicole Show*, ANS blips back onto your radar with a vengeance. You're teaching full-time at Austin Community College and moonlighting as a waiter at the Aqua Vitae Café to pay your student loans and mortgage; and every colleague at ACC and every waitperson at the café seems to be talking about Anna Nicole's antics on reality TV. Each week on *E!*, a scantily clad Anna Nicole and her entourage have a new adventure, and a group of aspiring literary—and social—critics gets together at your house to watch the show, applying the theories of Jacques Derrida and Roland Barthes to the freewheeling frolics of ANS; her pet dog, Sugar Pie; her attorney/boyfriend, Howard K. Stern; her camera-shy son, Daniel; and various other family members, groupies, dentists, and decorators.

But while the other people in the room (your soon-to-be-ex included) laughingly deconstruct the life of Anna Nicole—ANS, buns in the air, crawling around her mansion floor after Sugar Pie ("Could this be Derrida's famed abyss?"), ANS in a Santa Claus suit giving her party buddies shots from an ice-carved replica of her own cleavage ("Barthes's classic battle of nature versus nurture?"), a teary-eyed ANS hugging her late husband's urn against her ample bosom ("The birth of a new white trash archetype: lashes to ashes, bust to dust?")—you just keep feeling sadder and sadder.

Finally, on October 7th, 2004 as the last episode to air unfolds, you feel something new: shame for all the nights you spent after that first *Playboy* spread dreaming of Anna Nicole's expert tutelage in the science of things physical. What ever happened, you ask yourself, to the girl with the wishing flower? You slip out onto the back porch, leaving behind the crowd of hecklers in your living room. And on that stormy night in your Austin backyard, as the cloud rack clears and the crescent moon seems to float among the tightly furled morning glory blossoms on your back fence, the ghost of Vicki Lynn Hogan flashes into being beside you—and leans in for a kiss.

Square-jawed, high-cheekboned, she is the polar opposite of ethereal. The whole world smells of river water, you feel cold wet skin against your skin, and terror courses through to the icy core of you. Until you manage to pull back, look into her eyes that stare straight through you—and feel your terror melt into bewilderment.

Anna Nicole Smith, you tell yourself, is still alive. How can the ghost of Vicki Lynn Hogan be manifesting, here and now, in your backyard?

As if in answer, the specter begins to fade. And you catch your first glimpse of the place she's staring into—a future that never should've been, but was.

4. *Consequences—Frio County, TX*

It's March 27th, 2007 and you're sitting on the back porch of the ranch house you grew up in watching the fiery orange ball of the sun sink below the line of hills that marked your childhood horizon. On your lap is an issue of *Texas Monthly* from a little over a year ago. Anna Nicole Smith is on the cover for another Bum Steer of the Year Award (her third or fourth, you've lost count). You've just heard the news that she is dead, and a witch's brew of emotions is coursing through you. Sadness.

Shame. Bewilderment. Responsibility, for the first time in your life, for the spectacle and its aftermath. As you glance back and forth between her photo on your lap and the distant sun fading red, you can't help but relive through the eyes of the media—media you patronized, subsidized, consumed—the lives of Anna Nicole and those around her falling to pieces over the course of the last year.

For Anna Nicole, 2006 unfolded with the birth of a new daughter, Dannielynn, followed hard upon by the death of her son Daniel in his mother's hospital room. Not long after the laying-to-rest of Daniel, Anna Nicole and what remained of the "family" were evicted from her Bahamian mansion for defaulting on the mortgage loan. All of this played out against the backdrop of a paternity lawsuit filed by photographer and ex-lover Larry Birkhead, challenging Howard K. Stern's and Anna Nicole's claims that Howard fathered Dannielynn (the paternity suit was settled in Birkhead's favor after her mother's fatal over-dose).

In many ways her writ-large struggles are a touchstone. Your own 2006 and early 2007 contained some of those same elements, if not the awful finality. You've been through an ugly divorce that cost you your house and your life in Austin, and moved with your son Jacob back to the ranch you grew up on; you've met a gorgeous and wonderful woman named Sara with a sprite of a daughter named Ariel who is almost six, and the two of them have stolen your heart; you're hoping to begin a splendid blend of a family. You've finished a book on the Latin Settlement in the Texas Hill Country that you're confident will land a university press, and you've scored a Visiting Assistant Professor gig at the University of Texas at San Antonio. Neither rich nor famous, you've begun to

realize that you have not much chance of becoming either one. But you're on the verge of achieving real success.

Aren't you?

As you stare into the blood-red remnants of the dying sun, you know for a fact that Anna Nicole would say no. But the question that really matters is: What about Vicki Lynn?

Then the scent of river water permeates the desert air. You feel a cold wet touch on the back of your neck, but no fear. As you turn to face her, the beginning evening hushes, expectant.

But her only answer is that distant stare. Gleaming softly in the gathering twilight, the ghost of Vicki Lynn Hogan rests a silent hand on your shoulder and the two of you watch the first bright stars wink into the dark.

5. *Legacy – Aiken, SC*

Back in the here and now of February 5th, 2021, you still don't have that answer. A department chair now, with multiple books and a beautiful blended family (two girls, two boys, a dog, and a cat), you feel like you've finally arrived. But something tells you that the life you've built would be a disappointment to a certain world-wise 12-year-old and her dandelion wish. You glance at Beatrice and Ariel watching *Entertainment Tonight*, at the ghost of Vicki Lynn Hogan staring in your window, at the face of Dannielynn Birkhead on your TV screen—and the question of what defines success suddenly seems as nebulous as the Milky Way.

You've spent your whole life trying to answer it. Reflecting on your own experience, and on Anna Nicole's. Poring over books and articles. Contemplating as best you could perspectives philosophical, historical, psy-chological, and sociological. Keeping company with the dead.

It occurs to you to put the question to your stepdaughter Ariel—who at age eighteen has blossomed into the same pale-skinned and dirty-blonde beauty as her mother Sara, but is in so many ways still a child. "What do you want to be," you ask, "when you grow up?"

"Famous," she says, without missing a beat.

"Wait a minute," you say. "I'm being serious. Isn't there anything else you want to be?"

"Rich," she says, and goes right back to watching *Entertainment Tonight*.

Beside you on the couch, 4-year-old Beatrice sits smiling at the face of Dannielynn Birkhead on the TV. Outside the window, the specter of Vicki Lynn Hogan isn't looking at you either. You follow her gaze, trying to catch another glimpse of that future place she's staring into, but the only thing you see is the ghostly reflection of the television screen.

Yes. No wonder of it. But what would happen if I let it be known that I talk with Trees?

Jerry Craven

Angelic Embrace

Angelic Embrace

Jerry Craven

Rosita told the Painter you must
dip brushes in velvet orchids to paint the queen
in dewy odors of sapote beside the sheen
of labios calientes infusing passion in serene
blessings for our river jungles' dying green.

Take angel colors from our ride on Rio Churun,
Rosita said, paint her face with parrot pink
and red papaya moist on her cheek,
with azul like Sam's good eye that might
have found its blue in a distant Texas sky.

Make her arms green-and-red-smeared paint
streaked into her embrace, but paint divine arms
unlike ours, then sprinkle her face with light,
with ruby and citrine crystals, with diamonds, all
from a salero, and give her labios calientes;
take the hot lips from leaves of the bush
psychotria, beloved of hummingbirds,
to make her human and not human, and shape
her face like Sylvia's before the shotgun murder.

Make this Angel Sylvia a living and holy
curadora wrapping her star and gemstone skin
around all of America del sud, and paint her eyes
closed in her warm embrace from living leaves
to bless the faded jungles into green again.

But already, I feel the tingle of new growth
in my shoulder blades. My metamorphosis is
Underway.

Andrew Geyer

Woman on a Rock

Woman on a Rock

Terry Dalrymple

You know that person you once saw briefly, the one whose image you can't forget? Mine's a woman on a rock by a beach up in Maine. I was twenty-one, a Texas boy fresh out of college, and I drove with a friend five thousand miles there and back, and all I remember from that trip is a woman on a rock by a beach up in Maine. I don't know her name, I never saw her face; but three jobs, one marriage, and two kids later, I still can't forget the woman on a rock by a beach up in Maine.

She's young and lean and I believe she's beautiful, and her long blonde hair is pulled into a ponytail, and her shirt is loose, and her pants are tight, and in her high-top tennis shoes she rocks my world. She faces the heavens with her hands held high as if she's conducting the music of the dark universe above and the lightning veining toward the vast water below. And I know I love her and love her forever and will never forget that woman on a rock by a beach up in Maine.

The ancient ones always knew that the soul stamps itself upon the body. Morality and beauty are essentially the same.

Jerry Craven

8. Shifting Plumage

So Many Lovely Lies

So Many Lovely Lies: A Study of Irony in 7 Quotations, 2 ½ Suicides, and 1 Broken Heart

Andrew Geyer

1. *Except for music, everything is a lie, even solitude, even ecstasy.*

Romanian philosopher Emil Cioran wrote those words in 1987 at the age of seventy-six. He spent his whole adult life—and his entire philosophical career—contemplating suicide, but died of natural causes at the age of eighty-four.

Life is irony.

As it turns out, much of my adult life has been a case study, testing whether Cioran's statement about music and about lies is as true in the world of Forms as it is in the world of Ideas. For the majority of that time, I was an unwitting lab rat—running through my maze each day, savoring the reward at the end of my path, blissfully unaware of the grand experiment in which I played such an integral, albeit unconscious, part. Only in the past six months has my role become purposeful. Considered. Conscious.

Ironically, the series of events that woke me up resulted in the death of my wife. The medical examiner ruled that her death was accidental, but I know otherwise.

2 *Pain is inevitable. Suffering is optional.*

Haruki Murakami, the Japanese author and distance runner, wrote that, and I contemplate the distinction as I jog through the snow.

Is there a real-world difference between the two, I wonder—an otherness that does not involve the semantic acrobatics of Buddhism? The icy air in my lungs is painful. And because I haven't eaten in twelve hours, I am suffering

hunger pangs. But how is the pain in my lungs different from the suffering in my belly? Or, for that matter, the blisters on my toes?

As I approach the intersection of Marlboro and South Boundary, and the red light of the rising sun glitters on the ice-crusted asphalt beneath my feet, only one thing is certain: I am about to put Murakami's philosophical statement to a real-world test.

It is a perfect morning for worldview-testing.

The great ice storm of 2014 pummeled Aiken, South Carolina all through last night; and like the battered remnants of my previous life back in Tulsa, Oklahoma, South Boundary Avenue is in tatters. The power lines are down, the great limbs of the venerable old oaks are down, the wreckage is covered in snow and ice. The red sun rises like a bloodshot eye. And yet, "Clair de Lune" by Claude Debussy floats in all its delicate elegance through my ear buds and into my brain, and as I pass the Marlboro stop sign and start across South Boundary, instead of pausing to look both ways, I close my eyes and keep running.

"Please, please," I pray to Buddha, to Jesus, to whatever higher power might be glancing my way, "let today be the day."

The pain in my lungs and the suffering in my belly blend, in a perfect contrapuntal melody, with the Debussy in my brain and the poignant anticipation of blunt-force trauma that fills my soul. And I reach out to embrace the afterlife, or eternal darkness, whichever the case may be . . .

But finally, instead of the bone-crushing

impact of an onrushing motor vehicle, I feel my feet crunch onto the mix of sand and snow on the far side of South Boundary. In the absence of a deus ex machina, I open my eyes. The rising sun brightens from bloodred into orange, from orange into yellow. And I continue on into the Aiken horse country and the emptiness of another day without Isabella.

3. *Man does not control his own fate. The women in his life do that for him.*

Groucho Marx, who was a master of irony, said that more than once. Groucho's actual given name was Julius, and all three of his marriages ended in divorce. I don't know whether Groucho ever contemplated suicide. But he did spend more than a decade hosting the game show *You Bet Your Life*.

Like Groucho, my own given name is Julius. And I bet my life every morning at the intersection of Marlboro and South Boundary.

Unlike Groucho, I have had only one marriage. It ended when the SUV my wife was riding in flipped over the guardrail of the Wilson Avenue Bridge in Tulsa, plunged into the Arkansas River, and sank like a stone.

If this were a different kind of story, a tale of true love instead of tragic irony, I might go on for pages about my wife's eyes. They were the color of blue ice, with an interior light like the snow that falls onto a glacier, is compressed, then becomes a part of the floe. I might tell you about standing with my wife on the deck of a boat on Lago Argentino in southern Patagonia—Isabella was Argentinian —and looking back and forth between the Upsala Glacier and her irises, which were exactly the same heart-piercing shade of deep blue and every bit as luminous.

Instead, I have to tell you that my wife was not alone in the SUV when it flipped over the

guardrail and plunged into the river. And I have to tell you that the man who died with my wife was in fact her lover, and had been for years—a fact I'd discovered only hours before.

4. *The imagination is the only thing worth a damn.*

The poet Hart Crane wrote those words. He committed suicide by leaping from the deck of the steamer *Orizaba* into the Caribbean Sea. He had just left the cabin of his lover, who was also the wife of his best friend.

Since the death of my own wife, and the series of revelations that preceded it, I've spent a lot of time imagining. Instead of the man she died with, who also happened to be my best friend, I imagine that it is my own naked body intertwined with the pale and lithe body of my wife—the body of an avid runner, although classical piano was her first passion—the throes of our lovemaking so intense as we speed across the bridge that we lose control of the Honda Pilot and literally take flight, spinning wildly through the air until the moment of impact with the water.

Unlike my wife, the body of the poet Hart Crane was never recovered.

But like Isabella, he must've died by drowning. Again and again I imagine smashing through the surface, the white-hot shock of impact fading as I sink deeper and deeper into the grip of the suffocating dark.

If this were a different kind of story, I might share with you the details of the afternoon my wife and I spent at Iguazú Falls, on the Argentinian side at Puerto Iguazú. It was our honeymoon. Isabella wore a loose-fitting white dress, short and sheer, and the wind— heavy with mist from the cataract—gusted up, billowing the dress around her thighs, her waist, her perfect breasts. I might describe to you the way the fabric became transparent as it clung to her skin, the way the sight of Isabella made me feel so completely alive and in love that I wanted to celebrate our honeymoon forever.

But this is not a story about celebrating life. It's about trying to find the courage to die.

5. *In the beginning was the Word, and the Word was with God, and the Word was God.*

John the Evangelist, who was the only one of the twelve Apostles not to have been killed for his faith, wrote that. Like John, I believe that words have the power to create and to destroy. Also like John, I am living out the end of my life in exile.

Unlike John, I do not reside on the Island of Patmos in the Aegean Sea. Instead, I've come to the city of Aiken in the state of South Carolina. The Atlantic Ocean is hours away. But as was the case with the Book of Revelation, and the Fourth Gospel, I am writing a tale of betrayal and its consequences for both the living and the dead.

Words created the life my wife and I shared back in Tulsa. My words, in a way, since I owned every book in Twice-Told Tales—the best used, rare, and collectible bookshop in the state of Oklahoma—and I made my living selling them. Online mostly, to collectors, although walk-ins were always welcome. I had decided that the best thing a failed poet can do is sell the words of his betters, and it was a good enough life. But lonely. Loveless, except for the passion in the lines of the masters, pressed into the volumes of poetry that took up an entire wall of my store.

That is, until Isabella walked in.

Night after night, in dreams, I relive the icy December morning when she first jingled the string of antique sleigh bells on the front door. Red-haired. Pale-skinned. Exquisite. Her eyes the most intense shade of blue I'd ever seen, and that I had no name for—she had not yet taken me to visit the Upsala Glacier—except *mesmeric* as she stepped up to the counter and transfixed me with her stare.

"Could you recommend for me a book of poetry?" she asked, without a greeting and in a lilting Latin American accent whose country of origin I couldn't place.

Instead of answering, or asking, I recited "Body of a Woman" by Pablo Neruda. In English, unfortunately—I had not yet learned to make love in Spanish—and then I gave her as a gift the book it came from: *Twenty Love Poems and a Song of Despair*. Although Neruda wrote the words, and M.S. Merwyn translated them, it was I who presented them to Isabella as though they had been created for her alone.

It was the beginning, and she was my Word made flesh.

I closed the shop and discovered over espresso at the coffee bar across the street that her name was Isabella, that she was a concert pianist and a professor in the School of Music at the University of Tulsa, that she was from Mendoza in the Andean foothills and her father made wine. Much later, after dinner at Mahogany Prime—Tulsa's best surf and turf—she played *Suite Bergamasque* for me on the grand piano in her living room. We were sharing a second bottle of Argentinian Malbec from her family vineyard, and although it was Debussy who wrote the music, based on a poem by Verlaine, it was Isabella who performed the "Clair de Lune" movement as though it had been summoned from the void in that moment and divided from the darkness to haunt my dreams until the end of time.

The words that destroyed our lives

belonged to Isabella. I read them on her computer in the aftermath of a temper storm. I'd been sitting in our living room, sipping Malbec and indulging in my second greatest pleasure, which was watching and listening to my wife play piano—to play an instrument, in Spanish, is to *touch* it (*a tocarlo*); and when Isabella played the piano, she made love—when *boom!* the sheet music went flying. Isabella could explode without warning when she was struggling with a difficult piece. And as I gathered up the scattered pages of Brahms's *Piano Concerto Number 2 in B-flat Major*, which she'd just flung at me on her way out the door, a series of unfamiliar notes sounded on her open laptop. I investigated.

What I discovered was my own personal apocalypse. Make no mistake: I died that day. Although somehow I find myself still breathing, inexplicably, half a continent away.

This being the kind of story that it is, I would gladly share with you the contents of the love letters I found on Isabella's laptop, in an email account I never knew she had. Addressed to a man I trusted, they stretched back for years. But the only thing that really matters, as I write this, is that the deeper I delved into the intimate details of the torrid love affair between my wife and another man—a man I'd introduced her to—the more the heat of their hunger for each other burned away my capacity for compassion. For conscience. Even for reason.

I lurched out of our house into the August heat, hauled a lug wrench from the toolbox in my old Ford truck, staggered six blocks to the restaurant that my now ex-best-friend owned near campus. And I loosened the lug nuts on the front passenger-side wheel of his Honda Pilot.

6. *Love is the heart of everything. If it stops working, all the rest withers, becomes superfluous, unnecessary.*

Vladimir Mayakovsky, who was the leading poet of the Russian Revolution, wrote those words in a letter to his lover, Lilya Brik. Lilya's husband, Osip, was Mayakovsky's publisher and friend. After a row with another married lover, Mayakovsky committed suicide by shooting himself in the heart.

Unlike the poet Vladimir Mayakovsky, I do not possess the courage to point a loaded gun at myself, much less to pull the trigger. I don't even have the guts to leap from the deck of a ship like the poet Hart Crane. Indeed, as has been the case so far with suicide, it may be that my failure as a poet was really a failure of nerve.

But like Mayakovsky, I do possess an intimate appreciation for the meaning of the word *irony*.

So I get up every morning, run to the corner of Marlboro and South Boundary, and close my eyes. In the endless seconds while I float between life and death on the ethereal notes of "Clair de Lune," I relive the moment that I discovered Isabella had been in my ex-best-friend's Honda Pilot when the front passenger-side wheel buckled and the SUV flipped over the guardrail and sank to the bottom of the Arkansas River.

This is what I always see:

Evening is falling. I am staring out the window at the darkness enveloping Tulsa and trying not to feel. Then a cop walks into my bookshop. A female cop, I see, and as she approaches the counter, it comes to me that she is here to arrest me for vandalizing the SUV of my ex-best-friend. Instead, she shows me a photograph of my wife and asks whether this was Isabella.

Was, she said. Even as a failed poet, I was familiar enough with the intricacies of the past tense in English to understand that Isabella had died. I don't remember what the cop said after that. What the words were.

But the photo:

The skin that was so pale in life is in death even more so, with the bluish tinge that comes from asphyxiation. Mercifully, someone has closed her eyes. There is a cut on her forehead and another on the bridge of her nose—from the dashboard? the windshield?—but both cuts are bloodless, so that they almost look drawn on.

I was struck dumb. Aphasic. Out of my mind.

I don't know how long. Instinctively, I walked over to the poetry wall. I pulled a pale yellow volume from the shelf and stared dumbly at the cover. A minute? An hour?

When I finally opened the book, I found a one-way bus ticket from Tulsa, OK to Aiken, SC. The ticket was like a key, unlocking my ability to understand words. Context. I realized that the ticket was a bookmark. The poem whose place it saved opened with the words *The lilacs wither in the Carolinas . . .*

The ticket, dated 17 August 1969, was long expired. Never used. I shut the book and read its title: *Harmonium*. I remember thinking about irony as I carried the book back to the counter and sat down.

7. *All that is solid melts into air.*

Karl Marx wrote that in 1848, in Chapter 1 of *The Communist Manifesto*, and revolutions broke out across Europe when people read it. For those readers who realized the full import of Marx's words, religion died.

The thing that died for me was love.

I suppose revolutions can either be about an ending, or a new beginning, depending on which side you're on. 161 years after Marx wrote them, I heard his words spoken aloud in Spanish by my wife. Although I didn't realize it at the time, her quotation marked the beginning of the end for my whole world.

It was the twenty-ninth of December in the year 2009, a day I thought was perfect. I had just finished the greatest run of my life, a sixteen-mile fast loop through the snow in Tulsa, a tune-up for my first marathon. I'd been running along the Arkansas River when a flock of Canada geese startled up off the water, circling around and above me through the snow that fell thick. The white snow swirled earthward, the geese whirled skyward in black and grey, and as I ran along in the vortex of their opposing motions, the planet itself seemed to slow. Time faded like my footprints in the snow, and I felt like I was running on air.

I reached the house, cold and wet and exhilarated. Breathlessly, I told Isabella about the geese and the snow and the running-on-air feeling. She warmed me by making love to me in her native tongue. But when we finished, she looked through me with those eyes like the icy Upsala Glacier and said, "*Recuerda.*"

"Remember what?" I asked.

"*Todo lo sólido,*" she said, "*se desvanece en el aire.*"

At the time, I thought she was talking about my run. But three years and eight months later, as I stared at her open laptop, having worked my way back to the very first of the love letters my wife had written to the man I thought was my best friend, I did indeed remember: *All that is solid melts into air . . .*

The letter was dated 29 December 2009. While I was running on air next to the Arkansas River, they began their affair.

Late in the evening of 16 August 2013—the

day I drowned Isabella—I read from cover to cover the book of poems that I'd pulled from the shelf by instinct after discovering my crime. *Harmonium*, by Wallace Stevens, perhaps the most ironical twist in this tale of tragic irony.

A *harmonium* is a reed organ with a foot bellows: it has the keyboard of a piano, but it runs on air.

Having realized for myself the full import of Karl Marx's words, I have not much use for organized religion anymore. But fate is another matter. The day after Isabella's funeral, except for my books of poetry and a select few works of philosophy, I sold all that was mine to sell. All that was hers went to Isabella's family in Mendoza. I loaded the remaining books, some clothes, and a few personal effects into my old blue Ford. Then I drove to Aiken, South Carolina, and bought the last house I will ever own.

I found it on Newberry Street, a two-story Colonial Revival fixer-upper built in 1887 with ten white columns on the front porch. The columns are of the Ionic order. The house has yellow siding and a red roof; the outbuilding in back, also yellow, has garage doors instead of columns and too much storage space for a man who came to South Carolina with all his worldly belongings in the back of an old Ford truck. But there is a pharmacy two doors down, and a family medicenter on the far side of the back fence. So if I work up the nerve to overdose on opioids from the pharmacy, and fail, help is across the fence.

I settled in, drank red wine, read poetry and philosophy. I found a liquor store called Harvard's that carried Isabella's family Malbec. I bought a laptop computer and installed WiFi. I drank a lot more wine. But for the life of me, I couldn't work up the guts to do myself in.

Finally, after a couple of months of self-loathing, while I was reading an article on the web about suicide machines, a car roared past the house on Newberry Street. I glanced out the front window and saw the Ionic columns on the front porch, and the idea for my deus ex machina was born. Later that day, I bought a cell phone and ear buds, and learned how to put Debussy's "Clair de Lune" on an endless loop.

The next morning, I started writing and running again.

I couldn't run very far at first. But I kept pushing myself, jogging a little farther each day and looking for the perfect intersection. It couldn't be too busy, or I'd lose my nerve; but too empty would be a waste of time. I settled on Marlboro and South Boundary, and I learned how to run with closed eyes.

Every morning, very early, I open up the laptop and work on this tale of love and betrayal—of collateral damage, heartbreak, homicide. I keep trying to find the perfect form to fit my story. It feels like more than a confession, but less than a Greek tragedy. A tragic hero must be noble, after all, larger than life. A poet or a warrior or both. And of course, I am as incapable of verse as I am of suicide.

But rosy-fingered dawn is reaching into the front windows now, turning the Ionic columns into prison bars. The time has come again to put aside the laptop and pull on my running shoes. Perhaps, at long last, today will finally be the day.

But as I clip on my cell phone, and send "Clair de Lune" looping endlessly through my ear buds, only one thing is certain: love dies, love dies, love dies.

The Birds of Scotland

The Birds of Scotland
Jerry Craven

A tree frog watched in red-eyed alarm
    the rowboat steered by a loon
unloading birds in a colorful storm
    and a duck put its feet on a moon.

They came in a rowboat now moored and damaged
on the edge of the loch beside a Dornie schoolhouse,
a mere stroll from Eilean Donan Castle.
Today caught in shallow earth waters,115117
boards shrinking, the loon and the yardbirds
long fled, that cosmic rowboat with eyes sagging
into age watches a cormorant holding wings
to dry, a robin perched on a pine finger,
a crow speaking to a rooster behind a moon.
Today the cloth swans of Dornie told me
about stars along the trip from Andromeda,
and the gray duck claimed she saw that very crow
swallowing the red-eyed tree frog.
The brewer's blackbird, its golden eye
winking, said all Scottish birds came
from the one rowboat rotting in Loch Long.
But they still come, the birds of Scotland,
for I have seen them arrive at Bonnie Prince
Charlie's Culloden House at Inverness,
fluttering new from the Sunday morning pipes,
singing, all of them, even ducks
whistling high notes conjured into
avian throats when the piper blew and squeezed
and fluttered fingers, delivering into Scotland
birds to carry their cosmic songs and settle
like feathers on the long Culloden lawn.
The older Scottish birds spoke of danger,
voices like bricks, warning new bagpipe
singers not to fly across the truck
rumbling highway to fields where Jacobite blood
flowed by English muskets and murdering cannon.
I wept from painful tales told by descendants

of that Dornie boat while bagpipe new-born
birds drifted into long notes of silence
on the Sunday morning defeated Culloden green.

I don't know her name, I never saw her face; but
three jobs, one marriage, and two kids later, I still
can't forget the woman . . .   Terry Dalrymple

Egret Angel

Egret Angel

Terry Dalrymple

When I opened the door, an egret stood on my welcome mat, one of the few things too mundane for my wife to take when she left. The egret walked right past me and stepped on my right foot in the process. "Well," I said, "come on in."

A few feet inside, the egret stopped, raised one wing, and gracefully waved it as if to say, "Close the door." I left the door open. "I'm a little busy right now," I said. Not exactly but sort of true. I was between jobs. But the universe had been making so much noise lately that I actually was busy trying to sort and arrange the chaos I'd been hearing.

The egret waved a wing as if to say, "Come on over." It stood by a cardboard box that substituted for the glass-topped coffee table my wife took.

"Come on over," the bird waved again.

"I'm a little busy right now," I repeated.

The bird walked back to where I stood at the open door. It spread its wings and looked up at me as if to say, "Bring it in."

"Not a hugger," I said.

Egret shrugged and then embraced my knees with its wide wings. After a few seconds, it released me and stepped outside. My knees felt warm. Egret waved its white wing goodbye and walked away.

After twenty-two years of marriage, I hated living alone. I wanted to talk to my wife about Egret Angel, even though I knew she'd say I had lost my mind. That's what she said when I told her about the noise. Later, she filed for divorce. Her lawyers kept calling, calling, calling her with questions and suggestions. And they kept e-mailing me and sending me letters with question after question and demand after

demand. Sometimes, I wanted to scream, "Stop hollering at me!" But there was no one to scream at, just my computer or mailbox.

And all of that occurred in the midst of my professional failure.

Two days later, the egret knocked again. And again it walked right in when I answered the door, but it did at least avoid stepping on my foot. It strolled over to the cardboard box coffee table and waved a wing, an indication that I should join it there. Its gracefulness and the purity of its white wings struck me as unique, totally unparalleled, except, perhaps, by angels' wings.

I felt a little guilty about my dismissal of the egret on that first visit. The intensifying cosmic noise had definitely diminished my social graces.

I closed the door and joined the egret. I sat in the lawn chair that substituted for the leather couch my wife had whisked away. On second thought, mindful of my manners this time, I stood and pointed at the chair. "Would you like to sit?"

The angel-like bird shook its head. I reoccupied the lawn chair. Egret Angel took two slow and, yes, graceful steps to stand in front of me. It raised both wings in a sort of shrug. "So, what's up?" I thought it asked.

"The noise," I said. "Can't you hear the noise?"

It cocked its head in a "What noise?" sort of way. But I should stop saying *it*. I had become by then convinced that she was female. Probably because of her grace.

"So," I said, "I don't get many egrets stopping by. Are you selling something?"

Her eyes popped wide in surprise, and she

shook her head emphatically.

"Good," I said. "I'm a little tapped right now."

She made a soft sound in her throat, and I somehow knew it was an expression of sympathy. I told her thanks. Then she stepped to my knees and spread her pristine white wings, beckoning, I thought.

"Like I said," I said, "I'm not big on hugging."

Just as before, she shrugged and hugged my knees. Then she flowed to the door and stood waiting for me to open it. I followed her and opened the door. My knees felt warm.

Had I still been working, I would have called Bob Garrison, my best colleague friend, to talk with him about my egret visits, but since I got canned he wouldn't answer any of my calls.

I had worked at corporate headquarters for a national company I won't name for fear of repercussions. A few weeks before my wife had filed, my supervisor had slapped me with an impossible sales quota. I told him it was impossible. He said no, it wasn't impossible. I worked night and day, constantly on the phone and on my computer trying to reach the goal. But I missed it, as I had predicted, and he

canned me.

Three days after her last visit, Egret Angel reappeared at my door. I didn't offer the lawn chair. The noise and the spinning chaos often dizzied me, so I had to sit. She stood at my knees and spread her graceful wings. Twice before, I had failed her in the hospitality department, so this time I leaned over and accepted her embrace. It was warm, warmer than any hug I'd ever felt, including my wife's hugs when we were young and lean and strong and horny as rabbits.

When she released me, I could swear she smiled. How can a beak form a smile?

At the door, I said, "Thanks for coming," and then I thought to add, "You're welcome any time." She smiled again and nodded. She took two steps off my porch and, instead of walking away, stretched her wings and flew up and up and up until I could see her no more, not even as a tiny dot in the sky. I never knew egrets flew so high.

I spent the rest of the day dazed and sitting in my lawn-chair sofa. That night, I opened my door and looked up, hoping to see her somewhere among the summer stars. I did not see her. Nor, I realized, did I hear the din of the universe. ꞷꟽꞷ

On one of our forays into its dark depths, I catch sight of a stone slab . . .
— Andrew Geyer

9. The Hair of the Dog

Running Blind

Running Blind: A Tale of Guilt and Penitence, and (Maybe) Miraculous Rebirth

Andrew Geyer

1. *Fame is a vapor, popularity an accident, riches take wing; the only earthly certainty is oblivion.*

American newspaperman, author, and statesman Horace Greeley wrote those words; and although he is better known for another quote—one that set a generation in motion toward the western frontier—I much prefer this one. Unlike Greeley, who sought fame, popularity, and riches to his dying day, oblivion is my sole remaining earthly goal.

Much like Greeley, I was undone by the death of my wife.

But unlike Greeley, who followed his beloved Mary into the grave a month after she died of a fever, I find myself lingering on and on in the absence of Isabella despite my daily effort to make an end. Indeed, it was in pursuit of oblivion that I came east from Tulsa, OK to Aiken, SC. Not mere obscurity, mind you (which Greeley so greatly feared, and to which he was referring in his second most famous quote) but annihilation. Extinction. Suicide by car.

Every morning, when the first light of day pales the living room windows, I close my laptop—placing this story of my life on a (hopefully permanent) pause—then I strap on my running shoes, slip on my earbuds, set Debussy's "Clair de Lune" on an endless loop, and set out in search of my denouement.

Every morning, as I run down Marlboro Street into the red light of dawn that silhouettes the venerable old oaks, and approach the intersection of Marlboro and South Boundary Avenue, my daily round of Russian roulette begins.

Every morning, I pray. "Oblivion," I whisper. And again, "oblivion," my words rising misty-white as remembered sins into the blood-red sky. "Please, please, please."

Then I jog past the stop sign, close my eyes, and keep running . . . .

2. *All have sinned, and all fall short of the glory of God.*

The Apostle Paul wrote that in his *Letter to the Romans*. Some Bible scholars believe that Paul was referring to original sin and the punishment of death that God visited, through Adam, upon us all. Others believe that Paul was referencing personal sin—those acts of transgression we ourselves commit, and for which we are assessed the ultimate penalty on our own merits.

Does it really matter, though, whether I'm punished for my inherent knowledge of good and evil, or for the act of killing my wife? Either way, by the laws of the Old Testament God, death is what I deserve. But I lack the courage to do myself in. Hence my daily close-eyed jog into the intersection of Marlboro and South Boundary, and perhaps—depending on traffic patterns and driver awareness—into the hands of the Almighty (or a reasonable facsimile thereof).

If there is indeed a higher power—Old Testament, New Testament, or otherwise—then the unseasonably cold morning of 17 April 2014 is the day I feel His/Her/Its grip close on me at last. A sudden scream of brakes, followed closely by the blare of a car horn and an explosion of pressure and pain in my left side, pronounce the heavenly sentence I've been waiting to receive since I learned that Isabella was dead. And I feel myself flying.

Flying, flailing, spinning through the dark, I feel my left side on fire.

Thinking, strangely, not of life or death or even what comes after, but of the Apostle Paul—who was born Saul of Tarsus, then struck blind by a vision of Christ on the road to Damascus—I hit the ground and feel myself rolling over and over, and it comes to me that I have been struck blind also. But when I'm brought to an abrupt, painful stop by what feels like one of the century oaks lining South Boundary, I remember that my eyes are closed.

I open them, like Paul, onto a bright white light. But instead of the face of God, I find myself staring into the headlamp of a banana yellow Land Rover. The SUV has skidded off the road and come to rest against the next in line of the massive oaks whose arching branches make the avenue a tunnel of green. The Land Rover's engine is still running, one of its high beams blazing. The other has been shattered, I assume by contact with me.

Beneath the engine's roar I make out a keen of grief, or pain, or both. I realize, dully, that my earbuds are missing—and that I am, tragically, still in the land of the living. The source of the keening sound is lying beside me, I see. A dog. Black and white and brown. And female. She looks like a Border Collie mix, but her skin on one side has been ripped open. I can see the musculature covering her ribs—pinkish red, like a rack of lamb in a butcher shop window—and I connect the keen of grief and pain with the terrible injury the SUV has obviously inflicted on the dog.

Then the driver's side door swings open and a woman jumps out, apologizing, asking me if I'm okay, saying that she only brushed me. Saying other things. There seem to be ten of her, a blur of sight and sound and motion. Helping me sit up, brushing off the dust and twigs, telling me that she is taking me to the hospital.

Instead of rising, I lean my face down close to the dog's. Her eyes look as strange as I feel. But farther away. One of the SUV's tires has rolled over her, it comes to me, and she is in shock. And fading fast.

The realization snaps my world back into sharp focus.

"—saved your life," the Land Rover lady is saying, "that dog. If I hadn't swerved to miss it, I'd have hit you head-on. And you'd be the one dying. Now let's go."

"Not *it*," I say. "*She*." Despite the cold early morning air, I pull off my sweatshirt and carefully wrap the shirt around the dog. "The dog is obviously female. But I don't see a collar. Do you have any idea who she might belong to?"

"The only thing I know is that I'm driving you to the hospital. Right now."

"Actually," I say, "you're driving this dog to the vet. Or I'm carrying her there."

So the woman who side-swiped me, and ran over the dog who saved my life, drives us hell-for-leather to the vet. On my lap, wrapped in my shirt, the dog lies very still. She is still making that awful sound, but so softly now as to be barely audible; every time her chest rises, I feel a sick certainty she's drawing her last breath.

"The vet's office is close," the Land Rover lady says, as if reading my mind. "Aiken Animal Hospital. It's just across Pine Log on Banks Mill."

We roar into a parking lot about a mile and a half from the accident site, if my distance-runner's inner odometer is to be trusted in my current distracted state. And to my surprise, there is already a vet in the office—a young woman whose name I don't quite catch. The Land Rover lady does all the talking.

The vet leads us into a small examination room where she gives the dog a shot, stitches the skin on her side back together, fastens a cone around her neck so she won't pull out the stitches, and tells me to give her wet food for a week or so. Then I'm supposed to bring her back to get the stitches out. It all seems to happen very fast.

Suddenly I find myself standing at the cash register in my running shorts and no shirt, holding the newly sutured dog in her semi-transparent pink neck-cone, and realizing that I have no way to pay this very nice young woman vet whose name I don't know for saving the life of the dog who saved mine. "Um . . ." I begin. But I have no clue what to say next.

"Excuse me," I hear over my shoulder, and the Land Rover lady gently nudges me aside. "I've got this."

"I don't even know your name," I manage, finally. Then I look across the counter at the vet. "I don't know yours, either." It's a stupid thing to say, much less repeat. But in my defense, it has been that kind of morning.

"Ana," the Land Rover lady says simply. As though I have not just said the most idiotic thing since *Let them eat cake*. As though she also realizes what kind of morning this has been.

As though she might actually be a very nice lady, despite the mishap involving her SUV. Then she pays the vet.

3. *You will witness a miracle.*

I have no idea who wrote those words. I read them on a slip of paper I pulled from a fortune cookie in Tulsa. It was the morning after the first night I ever spent with Isabella, and we ordered delivery from Mandarin Taste—Tulsa's best dim sum—and ate it, naked, in Isabella's big canopy bed. I remember the incandescence of her skin as I held the fortune in my hand—you will witness a miracle—and sunlight streaming through the sheer white gauze of the curtains like a blessing. I remember thinking about proposing even though we'd only known each other for a week. I had that slip of paper in my wallet when I actually did kneel and ask for her hand less than a month later. I carried it on our honeymoon through Isabella's home country of Argentina.

I have it still.

I assumed the miracle the fortune referred to would be the slow unfolding of our lives together, from glorious prime to vigorous middle age to the graceful fading of our later years, like one of those grainy old home movies shot on 16mm film. Instead I saw the lovely face of my wife, drowned, in a photograph. Killed in an "accident" I caused.

When I came east from Tulsa to Aiken in search of my ending, I slipped the fortune into a book of poems by Wallace Stevens: *Harmonium*. The poem whose place it marks is "The Snow Man." Like the title character, I have beheld *the nothing that is*.

Also like him, I *have been cold a long time*. And I am listening to the sound of misery. Still.

4. *Charity is the bone shared with the dog, when you are just as hungry as the dog.*

Jack London wrote that in a story entitled "Confession." Like Jack London, I am writing a confession of sorts. Also like London, my life has been changed by a dog.

The dog who changed London's life was the St. Bernard/Scotch Collie mix who served as the inspiration for Buck in *The Call of the*

Wild, the book that made its author a household name. For me, she is the Border Collie mix with stitches and a semi-transparent pink neckcone who gave me the idea that a second chance might actually be possible, even for someone like myself.

Instead of to the hospital, I ask Ana to drive me home. She takes the dog and me to my house on Newberry Street, a distance of about three and a half miles. We pull up in front of the house, with its ten white columns on the porch and its yellow siding and red roof, and she helps me get the dog inside. Once I'm settled on the couch with a blanket around my shoulders—I cannot seem to stop shivering—and the dog on my lap, Ana asks for my cell number and places her business card on the coffee table in front of me. Then she roars away in her SUV.

I look down at the dog. She looks back up at me with what appears to be a mix of love and trust, emotions I have not seen for so long a time in the eyes of another living being that I actually doubt my ability to recognize them. Love and trust had gone missing from my wife's glacier-blue eyes—perhaps a result of her infidelity, perhaps its cause—long before she sank to the bottom of the Arkansas River, naked, in my ex-best-friend's Honda Pilot. I look again into the brown eyes of the dog. They are groggy from the anesthetic, yes; but loving and trusting also, beyond question. And hungry, it occurs to me. Very hungry indeed.

Then it occurs to me that I have no dog food, wet (as recommended by the vet) or otherwise. No dog bed. No dog supplies of any kind. So I make a bed from a blanket and a cardboard box that I empty books out of—I owned a used bookstore in Tulsa, Twice-Told Tales, and books were about the only things I cared to bring with me when I came east—and I carry the dog, in her makeshift bed, into the kitchen. I scramble a dozen eggs in butter, and we share them straight from the pan. She licks hers from my fingers. I use a spoon. But we both eat as though each of us is starving. Next I give her water in a bowl that I hold in my hands so she doesn't have to try to stand. Finally I carry her back to the living room and start a fire in the fireplace, and as I watch her fall asleep on the hearth, my half-formed plan to seek out her owner fades to an utter impossibility.

Instead, I name her Grace.

Caring for her on this icy April morning has given me a sense of purpose, and of personal worth, for the first time since my attempt to punish Isabella's lover (and my ex-bestfriend) by loosening the lug nuts on the front passenger wheel of his SUV caused it to flip over the guardrail of the Wilson Avenue Bridge in Tulsa, plunge into the Arkansas River, and sink like a stone. If there is such a thing as the Grace of God—such a thing as forgiveness for those who have no claim on, nor any reason to expect, mercy—then the dog who saved my life and gave me a reason to keep living (at least until she heals) is a token of that grace. Semi-transparent pink neck-cone, stitches, and all.

Grace wakes up, midafternoon, whining for reasons I cannot fathom. But eventually it comes to me that she needs to go. I carry her outside into the front yard and hold her upright while she relieves herself. Then I carry her back to her box beside the fire. In the evening I feed her eggs again, this time with bacon, frying the eggs in the bacon grease and letting Grace have the whole pan to herself. I carry her outside again before bedtime.

I awake, long before daylight, on the couch beside her makeshift bed. My left side feels bruised and stiff—but unbroken—as I stoke up the fire, put on a pot of coffee, open my laptop, settle in to work.

Just as dawn is breaking, I hear a knock at the front door. It is Ana, dragging a giant bag of dry dogfood and with a sack full of wet dogfood in cans slung across her back. "You never told me your name," she says, as though showing up on someone's doorstep with enough kibble to feed a kennel is the most natural thing in the world.

"Julius," I say. Then I thank her for the dogfood, heft the giant bag up onto my shoulder despite the pain in my side, haul it into the kitchen. I pour Ana a cup of coffee and refresh my own. And we talk beside the fire.

Or rather, Ana talks. I mostly listen. And feed Grace some of the wet dogfood. It turns out that Ana owns a stable. Aiken is horse country—thoroughbred country to be exact—and Ana is a thoroughbred person.

She talks about horses next. Again, I mostly listen. And water Grace. Ana is only truly happy when astride her big bay jumper, she says, jumping. Or just riding him through Hitchcock Woods. Or grooming him, staring into his big brown eyes. He's getting older, though, she says. She doesn't know what she'll do when he dies.

The word *dies* is followed by a long and awkward pause during which we both stare at Grace. I am not a superstitious person; but I have felt the awful power of words to split our lives wide open, like the skin on Grace's side. To break the negative spell, I go to the kitchen, refill our coffees, return to the living room.

Ana is a widow, she says at last, looking away from me into the fire. She married a much older husband, a major player in the Aiken horse scene. Until he fell off his own thoroughbred jumper and broke his neck, she

says—a turn that makes further conversation impossible. At least, for me. I excuse myself and carry Grace outside.

To my surprise, Ana follows. "She needs to walk," Ana says, nodding at Grace, "to heal properly. And of course, to go to the bathroom."

"Of course," I say awkwardly, propping Grace up with both hands while she poops at my feet. When she finishes, I carry her back inside.

Instead of following this time, Ana fires up her SUV and roars away.

5. *To regret deeply is to live afresh.*

Henry David Thoreau, Transcendentalist essayist and poet—and also a great lover of dogs—wrote that in his Walden journal on 13 November 1839. Thoreau advocated looking forward instead of backward, turning life's mistakes and missed chances into wisdom, and using that wisdom to make a better world. Thoreau never married and was childless. In his journal, he portrays himself as an ascetic puritan. There is no evidence that he ever had sexual relations with anyone, woman or man.

Like Thoreau, I have become a great lover of dogs. Well, dog. As she has begun to heal, Grace has grown even more irresistible— dragging me around the property, sniffing her way into everything, showing me the world through her eyes. If I had her energy, maybe I could change that world like Thoreau.

Unlike Thoreau, I am neither an ascetic nor a puritan. But since causing the death of my wife, I have been chaste. I cannot claim chastity as a virtue, since mine comes as a result of blood guilt. Make no mistake: although killing Isabella was unintentional, her death (and the death of my ex-best-friend) resulted from an action I took with malicious intent—the fact that it was a reaction to their infidelity and lies cannot serve as a justification for their blood on my hands.

The ancient Greeks had a fascinating way of dealing with blood guilt, an expedient employed in Athenian courts of law after the sacrifice to Zeus of a plowing ox (the *Bouphonia* or ox-murder). It was felt to be a terrible thing to kill such a friend of man, and it was customary for all involved to be pros-ecuted, to blame each other in a fixed and ritual order, and finally to cast the blame upon the knife, which was thrown into the sea.

I am not a Greek, ancient or otherwise; and Aiken lies hours away from the Atlantic Ocean. So I make do with my daily attempts at suicide by car (put on hold until Grace has recovered completely), and with my vow of chastity. And of course, with Grace herself—by far the best part.

Once her stitches are out, Grace kicks the dragging and sniffing into overdrive—her cold, wet nose glued to the ground; her black-and-white-and-brown tail sawing the air; her once-gaping wound shrunk now to a bloodred ribbon of a scar that runs the length of her left side. Her favorite place to explore is my backyard outbuilding. Yellow like the house but with garage doors in front instead of a columned porch, it is a vast cavern of a place complete with cast-offs from the people who sold me the house.

On one of our forays into its dark depths, I catch sight of a stone slab behind a pile of leftover laminate flooring. It is just after dawn, too dark to make out much more than the headstone shape. But when we come back that afternoon, I bring a brush and a flashlight. Once I'm done removing decades worth of dust, and the light is shining on the face of the stone, the words I see carved into it make me sit down and stare:

The surname *STOREY* is centered across the top of the gray granite rectangle. At the lower right is written: *Mildred C. – April 14th, 1899 to September 23rd, 1918.* On the lower left is written: *Robert J. – March 15th, 1893 to*

"To what?"I wonder aloud, mystified. Riveted. But the rest is blank.

The fact that Mildred C. Storey died at the age of nineteen is crystal clear. But from what? Childbirth? The Spanish flu?

Also clear is the fact that Robert J. Storey lived on. But why would he have removed the tombstone from Mildred's C.'s grave and brought it here? One possible answer is that Robert J. married another woman, had another family—made more Storeys whom he chose to be buried among instead of lying down for his eternal rest beside Mildred C. The more I think about it, the more inescapable that conclusion becomes.

Why keep the old tombstone, though?

But of course the answer is obvious: regret. Obvious or not, thoughts of Robert J. and Mildred C.—and what came next for both of them—haunt me in the days and nights that follow.

Ana comes to haunt me too, but in a way that doesn't disturb my sleep. At least, not at first. It begins the day Grace has her stitches removed. Ana brings a gift, a leather chew bone that Grace immediately sets upon.

Once Grace is fully occupied, Ana looks me square in the face. "I have to ask you some-thing," she says. "It's important. I need a straight answer."

"What's the question?"

"I like to drive fast, I'll admit that. I'm damn good at it, never so much as a fender-bender my whole life. Until you ran out into that intersection, that is. I was mesmerized.

That's the reason I didn't swerve quicker—the reason I sideswiped you and ran over Grace. You were running with your eyes closed."

"That's not a question," I say. "It's a statement of fact. But I was indeed running. And yes, my eyes were closed."

Intense, rainforest green, Ana's eyes lock onto mine. "Why?"

Instead of speaking, I study Ana—really look at her for the first time, I mean—and consider what I see. She is smaller than I remembered, not more than five feet, with a thick mane of blondish hair that has been French braided. But the force of her personality makes her seem larger than life. Inescapable. "Are you familiar with the term *suicide by cop*?" I ask.

"That's not an answer," she says with an ironical half-smile. "It's a question. But yes, I'm familiar with that particular term. I live in South Carolina, for Christ's sake."

"Think of this as *suicide by car*."

"But . . . why would you want to kill yourself?"

"I'm a widower, you see. I find myself disinclined to continue breathing in the absence of my wife. But I want to go out on my own terms. In a manner that is neither too painful, too messy, nor too sure—one acceptable to a coward who lacks the courage to do the deed."

"Thank you for your honesty," Ana says. "Now may I be honest with you?"

"Of course."

"I find you more attractive, at this moment, than any man I've ever met in my life."

6. *History repeats itself, first as tragedy, then as farce.*

Karl Marx wrote those words in 1852. And although he was referring to the respective coups d'état in France of the Emperor Napoleon (1799) and the Emperor Napoleon III (1851), Marx might as well have been talking about the story of my life in Tulsa (1999-2013), followed by its sequel in Aiken, SC (2013-2014).

Like Marx, I'm a failed artist. Marx failed at fiction-writing; I failed at poetry.

My experiment with personal narrative is still a work in progress. But while it's certainly no Greek tragedy, I'm hoping that my story will rise above the level of farce and merit the term *tragicomedy*. Most often seen in drama, it can denote a tragic play with enough comic elements to lighten the overall mood, or a serious play with a happy ending.

While the jury is out on my own ending, I resolve to focus on Grace. And on Ana. Grace is doing splendidly. I take her everywhere now. She loves leaning out the passenger side window of my old blue Ford truck, her pink tongue lolling in the breeze, her brown eyes sparkling. We go for long walks in Hitchcock Woods. She has even begun running with me. Not too far at first, and slowly. A half-mile, then a mile, easy-careful—and nowhere near the intersection of Marlboro and South Boundary—but a little farther and faster every week.

As for Ana, she wants a romantic relationship. "Not an affair," she says in one of our daily talks over coffee. "I want us to be lovers."

The distinction is frankly lost on me. But I know better than to say so. Instead I tell her that since the death of my wife, I've been celibate. "What I really need," I say, "is a good friend." Here Grace gives me a questioning look with those big brown eyes. "A good *two-legged* friend," I clarify, and Grace licks my hand.

"I'll take that as a maybe," Ana says.

The next day, she takes Grace and me horseback riding in Hitchcock Woods. Ana rides English, on a gorgeous bay Thoroughbred stallion—high-spirited, huge, at least seventeen hands high. I ride Western, on a paint quarter-horse mare—short and fat and docile—that I strongly suspect is used to train child riders at Ana's stable. Grace bounds along beside us as Ana's big bay stallion prances and my paint mare plods, and I find myself belly-laughing for the first time in years.

"What's so funny?" Ana asks. We're riding along a wide forest trail that Ana has identified as Cathedral Aisle, and massive trees arch above our heads.

"I grew up on a cattle ranch in Western Oklahoma," I say. "We didn't own the place. My dad was the foreman, a hard-drinking, hard-riding SOB. If he saw me mounted on this Quarter Pony, he'd haul me out of the saddle and whip my ass."

Instead of laughing, Ana smiles. "So you grew up with horses," she says.

We stop for a picnic beside a lazy stream that Ana identifies as the Sand River. She spreads a plaid blanket, hauls finger sand-wiches and potato salad and utensils out of the saddlebags on my paint mare, tosses Grace a leather chewbone.

"So," Ana says, "sex." She hands me a bottle of pinot noir and a wine key. "It's no big deal. Anyway, it shouldn't be."

"It's always seemed like a pretty big deal to me," I say.

"It's the feelings people have for each other that really matter," she says. We eat the sandwiches, drink the wine. Neither of us touches the potato salad. Finally, Ana settles back onto her elbows and looks up at me. "You should learn to think of sex as an intimate handshake," she says, her green eyes sparkling in the dappled shade.

"An intimate handshake?"

"Absolutely. And I really want to shake your hand." Then she sits up, leans in, kisses me deeply. I don't know how long.

"I am incredibly attracted to you," I gasp at last, breathless, every part of me aching to do more than kiss. "But I took a vow of chastity. And as ridiculous as that must sound, I meant it."

"I'll take that as another maybe," Ana says, half-smiling that ironical smile.

7. *One must love with all of one's being, or else live, come what may, a life of complete chastity.*

George Sand, the French novelist and memoirist, wrote that. Sand, whose given name was Amantine Lucile Aurore Dupin, included among the list of her lovers Prosper Merimee, Alfred de Musset, and Frederic Chopin. The novel that made her famous, *Indiana*, is a protest against the social conventions that bind wives to husbands. Like Sand herself, the novel's title character abandons an unhappy marriage and finds love. Unlike Sand, Indiana makes a suicide pact with her lover. But they change their minds and live out their lives happily, after the death of her husband, on an island farm.

Ana comes over to the house in the evening after our ride. When I open the door, she hands me the saddlebags from our picnic. "Look inside," she says.

The first pouch is empty. In the other, instead of wine and finger sandwiches and potato salad, I find what looks like a leather feedbag that someone has cut the sides out of.

"A cut-up feedbag?" I say. "I don't under-stand."

"It's not a feedbag, it's a chastity belt. A gift from me to you."

I don't know what to say to that, so I don't

say anything at first. Instead, I study Ana's gift. The leather is dark red, the color of clotted blood or a fresh scar; thick, but supple. And soft. There are two metal d-rings, one on either side of the largest of the three openings. They look almost like the rigging dees on a Western saddle.

"Okay," I say finally. "I'll bite. Why did you bring me a chastity belt?"

"So that we can sleep together, of course. Without breaking your vow."

Without another word, she takes my hand and leads me upstairs. In my bedroom, we undress each other. Slowly. Calmly. Without urgency. I catch sight of Grace in the doorway, tongue lolling, head cocked to one side—a confused voyeur.

Once we're naked, Ana helps me pull on the chastity belt. She threads a silver chain through the d-rings, binds the chain around my waist with a golden lock, and hands me a key strung onto a piece of red ribbon.

I tie the key onto Grace's collar.

Then Ana and I climb into the bed. It's the first time in my adult life that I've gone to bed with a woman without at least the tiniest, most niggling intent of having sex. We hold each other very close, in a long embrace that is more than a hug but less than a love clench. We don't even kiss. Finally, Ana turns her back to me. I spoon her, awkwardly at first because of the chastity belt, but then the feeling becomes more and more natural. It isn't long before Ana is breathing slowly and evenly, smelling of horses, sunshine, Hitchcock Woods.

It is an entirely new experience for me. My relationship with Isabella was incredibly physical. There was intimacy, yes. But never without sex. I find myself thinking again about the Greek method of dealing with blood guilt— about knives and lug wrenches, and about casting blame into the sea. But the ultimate responsibility for Isabella's death has to rest on my flesh, and on my desire for hers: the jealous, possessive love that comes from a sex-based relationship. Despite my guilty feelings, I don't want to cut off my penis and throw it into the ocean. Could a chastity belt serve the same purpose? Do I want it to?

It's a night for difficult questions. Is there really such a thing as romantic love in the absence of sex? And if there is, am I capable of it? Toward morning, my thoughts return to the tombstone in the storage building out back. To Robert J.'s new Storeys. And as the first light of the coming day starts to pale the window, I slip out of bed. I walk downstairs, fire up my laptop, and finish part two in this story of me, not with a suicide (at least, not yet) but with a dramatic question:

Now that you know my story, will you unlock the chastity belt and help me make a new beginning; or else, please take Grace home with you and let me continue on alone in search of an end?

Then I carry the laptop upstairs and set it on the foot of the bed. I take a slip of paper and fold it in half. On the top half I write in red ink: *Ana*. On the inside I write: *I need an answer*. I untie the ribbon from Grace's collar and place the key to the golden lock inside the folded page, which I place in turn on the keyboard.

Finally I pull on a pair of baggy warmup bottoms and a t-shirt, and I take Grace for a long walk. The air is brisk for May, and the rising sun turns the treetops bloodred—the color of a chastity belt, or a freshly healed scar.

Coyote in the Window

Coyote in the Window

Jerry Craven

I located Alexandra Cavan in a painting. She showed up as a tiny figure in a protest march, painted, impossibly, under the spiked heels of a lady with beautiful legs.

I had assumed Alexandra changed her name and left Port Arthur so I could never find her. But there she was in a painting I bought in Salado. She stood less than an inch high on the canvas, right beside a man I thought had died, a bully I didn't like. Donkey Echecs.

The painting, "Coyote in Window," took me on a computer search for the woman with wonderful legs sitting in one window and a howling coyote posing in another. My search wasn't really for the coyote or the lady with pretty legs but for Alexandra who, many years ago, was the one I would love forever.

When a new web search for Alexandra turned up nothing, I ripped through the world wide web and found a photograph and address of the real house that someone had used for the painting.

It stood overlooking Sam Rayburn Lake in Texas and a forest of pines, magnolias, and sweetgums. Except for not being awash in stars, the house looked exactly like the painting, complete with coyote and lady in windows. Not possible, I muttered, and walked to the door.

A child in the guise of a priest stood glimmering and small inside the glass-walled living room. I knocked.

When he opened the door, the priest stood over two meters tall. He regarded me with an amused smile. "I'm Father Olmus," he said. "Shall I assume that Miss La Tappa is showing her legs again and that you want to have her?"

"No," I said. "I'm looking for Alexandra Cavan."

"I spoke with her perhaps two years ago. Three. She's here, literally on the second floor." He stepped aside and gestured toward the stairs.

As I moved past him, I asked, "Where is the kid in the priest robes?"

"Size, like time, is fluid here. Miss La Tappa might explain. Be careful of the coyote. She is sometimes large, and if she dislikes you, she will bite."

At the top of the stairs I looked into a room cluttered by what appeared to be small figures scattered across the floor. Miss La Tappa crossed her legs. "I'm retired," she said, "and I never did like the men who paid to take me."

"A priest downstairs said Alexandra is here."

"That's Father Olmus, and he isn't a priest. He's an artist." La Tappa scanned tiny figures on the floor. "Alexandra Cavan is right there beside the one who wants to be called Donkey."

Astounding, I thought: she knows names from my past. "Frank the Donkey Echecs?"

"Yes, Donkey Echecs. Talk with them if you want, but be warned that time is different for them. You might be hours down there, but when you return, only seconds will have passed."

I started backing out of the room, away from the lunatic retired prostitute with lovely legs when crowd noises startled me, and I nearly fell from bumping into Donkey Echecs.

"Wes," Donkey said. "Wes Boyd. You've aged."

But Donkey had not. Nor had Alexandra, who was the same beauty I knew years ago.

"Why are you here?" she demanded.

"In this room?" I looked around, saw no walls, saw a street full of people, some carrying signs denouncing police.

Alexandra looked disappointed. "You're not here for the march, are you?" Her voice carried a hard edge of accusation. "You're here to tell me you'll love me forever. *Forever*. What a stupid word."

"I did love you forever back then. I wanted to find you, to start another forever love. But this, this—" I waved my hand at the crowd around us, at the line of police a half mile ahead of us—"this is all wrong. I came here from a room in a crazy house, slipped back in time somehow, found you and Donkey here—"

"Together, you mean? Found us together. You never saw that before, never during all your saying you and I would always be together."

"Ha!" Donkey said. "You never learned that it's always wrong to say *never* and that it's never right to say *always*."

"You and Donkey?" I felt my knees grow suddenly weak, felt a pain in my stomach not unlike the one that knocked me down when Donkey struck me in anger, balling up his fist and swinging after I beat him in a chess game. In the Port Arthur library, I remembered in an absurd flash there in the midst of a protest march through a street too large to be in a tiny room inside a house above Sam Rayburn Lake.

"Yes," Alexandra said, her tone a mean taunt. "Me and Frank the Donkey together even in that library where you gloated about winning a silly chess game. Me and Donkey, and you never saw it. Go away, Wes, go back to Miss La Tappa who will tease you with her wonderful legs and refuse offers of forever love."

"I will," I muttered and pushed through the crowd toward the safety of that line of police. "I will go from you forever, flee your betrayal, run from any kind of love with you—"

That's when Miss La Tappa appeared, materializing as from a mist, taking my arm to keep me from falling on a floor cluttered with tiny figures.

"That was faster than most," La Tappa said.

"I don't understand." I hated my whiney tone.

She led me to the door, released my arm. "Ah, but you do. Leave now, and take care that our little coyote doesn't follow. She would like you now that you have some wisdom, but before long she would be nipping you."

I stumbled down the stairs where a tiny priest held the door open for me.

128

The Witch and the Dirty Dog

129

The Witch and the Dirty Dog

Terry Dalrymple

My girlfriend's a witch. Seriously. Bona fide. Certified.

So here's what happened: We'd been dating about a month. We were sitting on her couch watching a movie called *The Witches of Eastwick*. Pretty stupid movie, if you ask me. Anyway, she turned to me and said, "Hey, I'm a witch."

I said, "Aw, you're not that bad. Just a little bossy sometimes, maybe. And grumpy."

She slapped my arm. "You dirty dog."

The women on the tv were concocting some crazy magic stuff. "I told you about being a witch," she said, "because I think I love you."

"Oh," I said.

"Don't you have anything else to say?"

I thought a minute. "Nothing comes to mind."

She punched me in the gut. "You really are a dirty dog."

After the movie, we went to bed. For the first time since we'd been dating she wanted to do what couples often do in bed. After, she asked me how it was.

"Okay," I said. "I guess it could have been better."

She slapped my face. "You are a major dirty dog."

And then I was. A dog. A dirty dog. Hair all matted and clumped and rife with fleas, only about half a tail that had mange or something because most of the fur was gone. It looked more like a naked mole rat than a tail. And I smelled. I mean, I smelled bad.

We didn't date when I was a dirty dog. I mean, I've seen some kinky things in my life, even participated in a few. But a dirty dog and witch, even I couldn't go there. Still, when I couldn't find any nasty stuff on streets to eat, I'd slink to her apartment and scratch and whine at her door. She'd usually throw me some scraps and then shoo me away. Hey, it was something.

I guess I was a dirty dog for about three months, and let me tell you, it wasn't fun. Nobody likes a dirty dog. But one day when I went begging for scraps, my girlfriend threw me a steak bone. Then, instead of shooing me off she said some crazy stuff I didn't understand and waved her hands all around, and I was a man again. A dirty naked man with a steak bone in his mouth standing on the balcony of her apartment with a gaggle of little kids in the swimming pool below. I dove for her door.

She closed and locked the door and dragged me by my ear to the shower. "You stink," she said. So I cleaned up, but when I stepped out of the shower I still had no clothes. She said I didn't need any and took me to bed. Later, she asked me how it was.

I'd been daydreaming about possibilities. "Okay," I said. "Might be better with a third participant."

She boxed my ears. "You're a major asshole," she said.

Uh-oh, I thought. 

10. Baptism

The Magical Bunnell Place

The Magical Bunnell Palace

Andrew Geyer

"Ana," Julius says, "you are the great love of my life." He cocks a thin, dark eyebrow at me. "But we've been sitting on this dock for two hours now, and I'm starved. Either tell me what you brought me here to tell me, or I'm walking back up to the beach house and taking Mercy and your mother to dinner—and leaving you here."

What to say? My marriage to Julius would be perfect if not for two things (in addition to the stubborn streak in both of us):

1. his rejection of even the possibility of a supreme being or afterlife;

2. my refusal to allow our daughter anywhere near the ocean.

Of course, as with nearly everything on this destiny-driven plane we currently inhabit, the two are related. But Julius doesn't know that. I have a secret, you see: a skeleton in my closet both beautiful and terrible, comprised of good and evil in equal parts. There is a term for this—*agathokakological*—a word that my book-loving (and bookselling) husband would very much appreciate, except for one thing: he doesn't believe in good and evil.

Much less in fate.

For Julius, the force that drives our lives is irony. It's an argument the two of us have on a regular basis. For example, our marriage: I knew from the moment I sideswiped him with my banana yellow Range Rover that the two of us would wed (Julius is a distance runner; I like to drive fast—holy matrimony was our fate, plain and simple). "It was *destiny*," I always say. "More like *deus ex machina*," he always answers. And I roll my eyes.

Julius has a fascination with Greek tragedy, Greek poetry and philosophy, all things Greek. An entire wall of his bookshop in downtown Aiken, South Carolina is dedicated to translations of classical Greek texts, and he is the best-read person I've ever met. But that doesn't make him right about fate, or about good and evil.

Lived experience is truth.

The only living person who knows my secret is my mother. All the others have left this grayscale plane we live on for the Magical Bunnell Palace—where, bathed in the rainbow-colored radiance of the afterworld, they await me and mine. In addition to my mother, *mine* consists of Julius and Mercy, both of whom also deserve to know my secret. Mercy when she is a little older; Julius now, or very near to now (in response to the pointed ultimatum he just issued).

"Now or never," he says again, rising to leave.

"But . . . but the reason we're here on this dock, on the Autumnal Equinox, is something I've never told anyone," I equivocate, instead of answering. "Ever."

"So. The mystery deepens," he says and sits back down. Dark-haired, dark-eyed, with his dusky half-Kiowa skin, he scans the long wooden pier connecting the backyard of the Bunnell family beach house on Edisto Island with the boat channel that runs through Big Bay Creek and into the Atlantic Ocean. "And I thought the reason we were here was your Thalassaphobia."

"*Thalassaphobia*?"

"Fear of the sea. Specifically, your fear of falling into said sea and drowning—or even more specifically, of Mercy doing so."

Having grown up in a landlocked state

(Oklahoma), and being a grecophile to boot, Julius has an inborn hunger for the ocean. Me? I'm sitting in the exact center of the boat dock—the farthest possible point from the water that surrounds us—and it is all I can do to keep from digging my fingernails into the weather-beaten wood. Our three-year-old daughter is up at the beach house with my mother, about fifty yards behind the shoreward corner where Julius sits dangling his legs over the marsh. Mercy. She looks more like her father than like me: raven-haired, dusky-skinned. But with my green eyes. Those eyes, right now, are probably gazing out over the salt marsh that the pier runs through. Soon the sun will set in front of us, and the marsh and the creek will fill with orange and red and gold.

"Wait a little," I say. "Until the sunset."

That gorgeous burnt-orange orb flashes in the windows of the sprawling beach house my Great-Grandfather Storey built, and bequeathed (along with the bulk of his other earthly possessions) to his granddaughter—my mother—who is sitting on the back porch next to Mercy. The "beach" house actually sits on the salt marsh side of the island, but Edisto Beach is just a five-minute bicycle ride away. My family has spent two weeks during the summer of every year since 1960 in this place, and those memories gleam in my mind like the sun in the windows behind me.

All of them, that is, except the one I'm here to share with Julius.

"All of me is rainbow," I say at last, as the sun sinks into the far side of the creek and everything around us seems to catch fire. For a moment the workaday world we inhabit is all aflame with the vibrancy of the world to come, and the two seem to inhabit the same space.

"Is that what you brought me here to tell me?" Julius asks.

"Part of it. I'm not sure whether it's the ending or the beginning, past or present or future. Maybe all of them at the same time."

"Okay, so all of you is rainbow. Was rainbow. Whatever. What comes next?"

"I'm five years old. Sitting right where you are now, on the salt marsh side of this dock. Then I stand up, and I leap feet-first into the water. But the tide is going out, and the water level is too low, and my feet get stuck in the pluff mud on the bottom. The surface of the water is just inches above the top of my head. At first, I try pulling my feet out of the mud; but the harder I pull, the deeper they sink. Then I feel myself starting to run out of breath. The surface glistens above me like the skin of a living sky. I can reach my hands up through it, into the air. I can feel *life* inches above me. But I can't breathe, and I can't get loose . . . I realize that I'm drowning . . . thrashing and splashing and gagging on saltwater . . ."

"Ana? Ana? Are you okay?"

"Until, suddenly, I'm . . . not. I'm standing on the dock and looking down at my hands sinking slowly into the brackish water. I see my bright blonde hair floating like the halo of an angel. I feel myself die. Then something spins me around. I turn and walk back up the pier to the beach house. I see the earth in miniature floating above the roof, spurting blue water. I see the moon in all four phases, and ringed planets. I see a giant orange fish swimming in the sky. As I open the gate at the top of the pier, what looks like the aurora borealis starts to flame up out of the roof in gorgeous green sheets.

When I walk into the house, my Great-Grandfather Storey is waiting inside, not only alive and well—even though he'd been dead for ten years—but young and spry, and he rushes to embrace me. The house is lit up like a magical palace, glowing, rainbow-colored. And so am I.”

“But . . . You’re here. Now. How could you have felt yourself die?”

“For almost five minutes, apparently, I was clinically dead. Then suddenly I was back inside my body, choking, throwing up seawater. It felt like my lungs were on fire. A neighbor had seen the whole thing from the dock next door and was bent over me, giving me CPR. He brought me back to life. Of course what I’d done was open the gate, sneak down the pier, and jump off the dock into the water—despite multiple warnings from my mother not to do exactly that.”

Julius is close beside me now, and I feel the warmth of his arm encircling my shoulders. “You mean,” he says softly, “you did just exactly what you’re so terrified of Mercy doing. Which is why you refuse to let her go into the ocean.”

“Precisely.”

“I am so sorry,” he says, “for my smart-ass *Thalassaphobia* comment. And for being so freaking smug.”

“How could you know? The only living person who did was my mother. And I made her promise not to tell.”

“I think I understand now why you brought me here on the Autumnal Equinox,” Julius says. “It’s Persephone, isn’t it? The descent into death, and the return. But instead of being dragged into the Underworld from a flowery meadow in Sicily, you drowned in a salt marsh on the South Carolina coast.”

“I think of Persephone every time I’m at the beach house. And yes, that’s why I brought you here today.”

“So does that make me Hades?” Julius half-smiles at me. “I guess I do have a bit of a dark side. And I can certainly see you as the goddess of spring.” Then the half-smile fades. “But Ana, the story of Hades and Persephone is a myth. This unreasoning fear you have of Mercy drowning is real. And you’re keeping our daughter from learning how it feels to play in the sea.”

“What happened to me was real!” I hear the heat in my voice. And as I pull away from Julius, I feel my cheeks start to burn. “I drowned, for Christ’s sake! How can you call my reaction to that an *unreasoning fear*?”

“I didn’t mean the drowning part. That was terrible. What I meant was that bit about the Bunnell family beach house being heaven, and your dead great-grandfather waiting for you there.”

“It was not a myth. I was there, and he was there with me. It felt every bit as real as drowning.” I expected Julius to disbelieve. That expectation is the reason I haven’t shared my secret with him until today—but surprisingly, staring that disbelief in the face, I feel my anger transform into a sense of inner strength and peace. “Listen,” I say, my voice calm. Reasonable. “I’ve been researching this for years. Dozens, if not hundreds, of near-death experiences have been documented. And many of those stories are virtually identical to mine.”

“Has any of that ever been reproduced in a controlled experiment?”

“Not exactly. But there have been veridical accounts.”

“For example?”

“Alright. One of the first cases I came across was a migrant worker named Maria who had a near-death experience during a heart attack at a hospital in Seattle in 1977. When she regained consciousness, Maria told her social worker that while the doctors were resuscitating her, she found herself floating outside the hospital building and saw a tennis shoe on a third-floor window ledge. The social worker went to the window and found the shoe—and the way it was placed meant there was no way Maria could've seen it from inside her hospital room."

The look on Julius's face is very much like the eye-roll I always get at the end of our arguments about destiny versus irony as the wellspring of our marriage. I feel the strong place inside myself start to collapse. And despite the promise I made myself before I brought him down to the dock to share my secret, I feel myself start to sob.

"Wait a minute," he says, his face softening again. "There's something else, isn't there?"

I'm sobbing too hard to speak, so I nod and glance back up at the beach house.

"Please, Ana. I'm doing my best to wrap my head around this. Help me."

I take a deep breath, wiping away tears. "It has to do with my mother," I manage. "When I was there in the Magical Bunnell Palace, and my Great-Grandfather Storey hugged me so tight, he whispered something. 'Take care of your mother,' he said. 'There's a bump on her cervix, and it needs to come out.' I told her about it, after. She didn't believe me

at first. But I kept on. Finally, she made an appointment and got it checked out."

"And the tumor was real?"

"It was small-cell carcinoma, a type of cervical cancer that is incredibly rare—and that usually goes undetected until too late. But they caught it early. My near-death experience was real enough to save my mother's life."

Julius's dark brown eyes meet and hold mine. "Tell me what you need from me to help make this better," he says.

"First, I need you to believe me."

"I believe . . . Hmm. I believe something happened to you, here on this dock, something beyond my capacity to comprehend."

"That's a start," I say. "A pretty good one."

"What else?"

"A simple compromise. You agree to go to church with me, just once, and I'll agree to let Mercy go into the ocean."

The look in his eyes goes faraway. "Just because I agree to go to church doesn't mean I agree to believe in what they're preaching."

"I know that," I say, and lean my head into the warmth of his shoulder. "And just because I let Mercy go into the ocean doesn't mean I'm not afraid of the sea. But it's—"

"A start," he says. "A pretty good one."

Green-Eyed Spirit

Green-Eyed Spirit

Terry Dalrymple

At midnight on January 9, her fifteenth birthday, Clarissa drowned herself in the local lake. But her angry, bitter spirit wanted revenge for all the wrongs she had suffered and so dragged her corpse from the dark water and resurrected her. As she felt life creeping back into her flesh, Clarissa cried out, "No, no, I don't want life. I just want peace." But her vengeful spirit was adamant, strong, and demanding.

* * *

Four days after she drowned herself, Clarissa Hovington stood at the worn wooden table in their kitchen, hands behind her back, glaring at her father. The man sat passed out at the other side of the table, his face pressed awkwardly against its surface. He reeked of alcohol.

"Father," Clarissa said. He did not move. She raised her voice. "Father," she said in an uncharacteristically angry, stern voice. He groaned and rolled his head to the side, but didn't rouse. She swung and slapped an open palm hard against his ear.

He groaned again, raised his head, and squinted at her with bleary eyes. "Clarissa? Where have you been?"

"I've a gift for you, Father." Her voice sounded flat, monotone.

"A gift?" He placed his palms on the table top and pushed up onto his feet. He swayed unsteadily. "You've always been such a good, sweet girl."

Clarissa swung her arms from behind her back, a butcher knife in her right hand. She clutched that right hand with her left, lunged across the table, and jabbed the blade into his groin. She cried as she finished up. The next morning, neighbors found him hanging from an oak limb in his front yard, the knife still lodged where Clarissa had aimed it.

* * *

Her mother died of pneumonia before Clarissa turned one. Her father first visited her bedroom shortly before she turned ten. Her older brother molested her not long after her twelfth birthday. A very handsome boy from school and the only boy Clarissa ever willingly allowed to have her laughed when she said she loved him. "Love!" he scoffed. "This don't got nothing to do with love." He never spoke to her again.

And so her life continued, boys taking advantage of her, always against her will, and girls playing dirty tricks on her and calling her by numerous demeaning and disgusting names, until that dark evening when she walked to a nearby placid lake and drowned herself.

* * *

Thomas Covington, Clarissa's older brother, sat in a tavern one hundred and twenty miles from where his father died, oblivious to his old man's fate. Earlier that same day, he had received a letter from the now-dead man saying only that Clarissa had disappeared, yet there she was, smiling at him from the tavern door. She beckoned to him, and he arose and crossed the room. "Clarissa," he said, "I'd heard you disappeared."

"I have something for you, Thomas."

"For me? What is it?"

"Not here. It's very personal. Come outside with me."

Expecting something he didn't deserve but had taken by force three years before, he followed her into the dark night. She led him to an alley, and when she turned toward him, tears streaked her cheeks.

In the early morning before the sun rose, a bum discovered him lying castrated in an alley but still breathing.

* * *

Throughout Clarissa's short life, everyone who knew her and many who saw her only briefly and from afar found her exceedingly beautiful. Her large emerald eyes nestled in a lovely face of blemish-free ivory complexion, framed by thick, wavy red hair. Other girls were jealous, and boys were desirous, especially when Clarissa reached puberty early and her breasts flowered. Even so, in all situations Clarissa behaved prudently, carefully, patiently. She was kind and humorous but shy, reserved, and unassuming.

* * *

Jimmy Druitt, the exceedingly handsome young man who had scoffed at Clarissa's admission of love, whistled as he walked home from an illicit meeting with his lovely, young school teacher. He took a shortcut through the woods, feeling proud and happy until Clarissa stepped from behind a tree ahead of him.

"Hi, Jimmy." She grinned at him, but the grin was not a happy one.

The boy gasped. "You can't be here," he stammered. "You're missing."

Clarissa stepped toward him. "I guess you found me." Jimmy stepped back. "Oh, Jimmy, don't back away. I have a surprise." She unbuttoned the top two buttons on her dress. "Do you want your surprise?" He grinned and lunged for her, and she wept as she tended to his punishment.

Later, when Jimmy stumbled through the door of his home, his bloody face was disfigured by dozens of deep slices, cuts, and punctures, and his tongue was missing.

* * *

Vicious harm came to twelve more boys or men and seven girls. No evidence existed to identify the perpetrator. Clarissa was still assumed missing, for no one had seen her except her victims just before their misfortunes.

Beginning with her visit to her father, Clarissa had resisted, and her resistance became increasingly vehement with each subsequent visit. Still, she could not overcome the demands of her spirit. But after she had attacked the last of those who had been most hateful and cruel to her in life, she said she was done. Her spirit said no. There were still many who would have abused her had they gotten the chance. They, too, were evil.

"Look at what I've done," Clarissa shouted aloud. "I'm evil."

Her spirit responded that justified revenge was not evil.

"I don't want revenge," Clarissa said. "I want peace."

"You're immortal. You'll never have peace."

"I don't want to be immortal."

"Too late."

"I will not seek more revenge!" Clarissa yelled.

* * *

Although other people in the area were occasionally victims of crime, evidence was always found and the culprit was caught. As far as anyone knew, Clarissa had simply disappeared many years before. Once every year or so, someone strolling by the lake at night claimed to have seen her out in the water or sitting on the shore and weeping. Once, a known drunkard swore he had seen her in the water, going under time and time again. Every time her head bobbed above the surface, he said, she screamed into the night, "Please, please, please." But everyone dismissed the old drunk's tale as a whisky-besotted hallucination.

I see him. Cleft-chinned, wild-haired, eyes afire with the glory of the music . . .
Abdrew Geyer

Dragged by Gold

Dragged by Gold

Jerry Craven

When the airplane dropped beyond its track

into the Hong Kong Bay

the general's wife went bubbling slack

down into the China Sea,

dragged by gold that weighed two stone

stitched into the leather band

that wrapped her slender waist.

Dragged by gold into the night

and anchored to the rocky sand,

the general's wife lies seaweed laced

and flashes green and gold and white

when the dead and crab-picked bone

catches rays from surface light.

11. The Vastness of Space

When Galaxies Collide

When Galaxies Collide

Andrew Geyer

1. *A cappella*

If Beethoven were the Angel of Death, he would separate my spirit from this timeworn body and bear me away to paradise at the end of "Ode to Joy."

If there even is such a thing as a spirit. And paradise.

Right now, I'm 99.9% sure. It's easy to believe in heaven when you're listening to a forty-voice chamber choir perform, a cappella, J.S. Bach's "How Brightly Beams the Morning Star." Even more so when you're conducting it before a rapt audience, the choir perfectly on pitch and in rhythm with the sway of your baton. As they are with mine now, during this first piece on the program of the 2019 Christmas Cantata at the Etherredge Center in Aiken, SC.

But later, when the program is over—after each piece has flashed into life, rippled through the sensibilities of six hundred gathered souls, and faded into the auditorium air—and I'm alone in my room at the B&B downtown, my confidence in immortality will wither. I'll lie alone in a rented bed and stare into the darkness. The stiffness of seventy-seven years on this earth will leach through my arms and shoulders down into my bones, and that .1% of heavenly doubt I hardly felt while conducting will balloon like the void between galaxies flying apart. And I'll be more inclined to agree with Prince Hamlet that *the rest is silence*.

Later, I'll poignantly regret not marrying and having a family. Family, after all, is immortality of a sort. And like Beethoven, I had my chance. My own Immortal Beloved.

I have known the ecstasy and the heartbreak of a woman's love.

But unlike Chopin, Debussy, and even Leonard Bernstein, all of whom made a hell out of the lives of the women who loved them, I chose not to hedge my bets by having children. I went all in on music, risked oblivion to live forever only in song.

I tried. Failed. Tried again, failed again—and not in the sense of Beckett's most deservedly famous quote: *Fail better*.

No, despite the swell of applause that greets the close of "How Brightly Beams the Morning Star"—and that continues to fill the auditorium long after the voices of the choir have gone still—I know that later, in the world outside these walls, the life I've led will not resonate beyond its final note.

2. *Azrael*

If Beethoven were the Angel of Death, this Christmas Cantata would be my swan song, this brisk midwinter evening the night of my rebirth.

It is the winter solstice: December 21st, 2019. And as I launch the chamber choir into the glory of Gustav Holst's "In the Bleak Midwinter," I am reminded that my own Viking ancestors called it Yule, the night the Goddess Frigga gave birth to the sun.

Out of darkness, light.

Ever since I was a boy, I've known that the Angel of Death is real and that his mission is to transport the souls of the departed. The People of the Book call him Azrael. But he has a thousand names, and the face he wears depends on whose spirit he has come to take. *Beautiful, terrible, jubilant, pitiless*: Azrael has appeared to me in all these avatars.

I grew up in Minnesota, studying piano

and singing in the church choir. The winters, with temperatures reaching sixty below, were especially hard on the old folks. When an Arctic blast blew through, some of the choirboys eyed the senior parishioners like vultures (if a rich one died, the family would hire us to sing at the funeral service). For me, though, it wasn't the money but the send-off that mattered: singing the souls along on their way to heavenly choirs—and a little later in life, playing them there. I made my orchestral debut at age twelve and immediately became the most popular funeral pianist in the Twin Cities. My rendition of Beethoven's "Moonlight Sonata" was on every playlist. Rightly so. If I could manage to play it perfectly (and only when I was perfect), the Angel of Death made himself visible to me. His countenance blazed like the morning star as he shepherded souls skyward, but swallowed up all light when he dragged them down.

After an incredible amount of study, and more than a little luck, I became a concert pianist. I performed at Carnegie Hall, Severance Hall, the Kimmel Center for the Performing Arts. I made three albums, the first of which won rave reviews. But the next two died on the shelf. After that I changed course, returned to my choral roots—and forty years of obscurity. At the end of this academic year, I'll be retiring from my position as Professor of Music at Furman University but remaining in Greenville, SC.

Obscurity indeed.

It was at Furman, though, that I met my Immortal Beloved—she who inspired me to achieve *the gorgeous range of musical colors* (in the words of *American Record Guide*) on that first album, and what I thought would be lasting fame. The record featured me as solo pianist playing songs of love. Magical songs. *Songs for Lucy*. After I let her go, I never

recaptured that alchemy.

But my Immortal Beloved is in the audience tonight.

As the Holst piece comes to a triumphant close and the listeners rise into a standing ovation, I turn, take my bow. And I focus all my gaze on Lucy, standing in the front row, looking up at me. She is in her sixties now; but in the afterglow of the stage lights, the years fall away.

I see her as she was then.

3. *Avatar*

If Beethoven were the Angel of Death, he would carry Lucy and me away together as the final word of "Ode to Joy" rises through the auditorium roof.

That final word, after all, is *dwell*. Something Lucy and I never did together. I ease the choir into "O Holy Night," remembering Lucy at nineteen. She majored in music at Furman and took piano from me. She was radiant, talented, ardent. Lithe. The first time we made love, we were like two galaxies colliding, all heat and light, a blazing cosmic ballet.

When galaxies collide, new stars are born. I translated the passion we felt for each other into piano music—arranged our appetite for each other into classical love songs by Beethoven, Schumann, Brahms, Bizet—and for a fleeting moment, one of those stars was me.

Then I was granted sabbatical leave for a concert tour, and a choice had to be made. In the excitement of that first flush of success, I chose music over love. But it wasn't only the siren song of achieving immortality through my work that drove my decision. I was thirteen years Lucy's senior, her professor; she was nineteen years old, my student. I was about to spend a year in constant travel and practice.

What else could I do but end our affair?

Two failed albums later, I made the change back to choir. But always, across the decades, I kept track of Lucy's life. She gave up her study of classical piano, changed her major to music education. After graduation she went back home to Aiken, married her high school sweetheart. Gave birth to a son who died and a daughter who thrived. Became a widow. A week ago, when I made the decision to end my career at Furman, I sent her a letter and a front-row ticket to tonight's Christmas Cantata. The letter opened with a quote from Hemingway: *No one you love is ever truly lost.*

And now, as the final chord of "O Holy Night" fades into the darkness and I turn to acknowledge the audience's applause, it is only Lucy I see. I wonder what she sees as she gazes up at me. An old man squinting through stage lights, looking half-dead in his tux?

Or does she, like me, see only what was?

I turn and send the choir careening into the final piece of the evening: the ecstasy that is Beethoven's "Ode to Joy." Forty voices intertwine, softly at first and then crescendoing through the auditorium like fireworks into the night sky. Perfect polyphony. And suddenly, in the darkness above the proscenium arch, I see him. Cleft-chinned, wild-haired, eyes afire with the glory of the music, the Angel of Death appears as Beethoven. He stands at my side, turns with me in triumph, accepts the applause that explodes as the audience springs to its feet.

We beckon Lucy together up onto the stage.

Shining like the crystalline firmament, she ascends the stairs. The applause is piercing the walls of the auditorium now, and I take Lucy's hand in mine. We arise together. Up through the roof and into the crisp clear Carolina sky, we are gently borne by Azrael. The full moon is a rainbow and Mars beckons us on, bright orange. Farther and faster now we are carried along past Jupiter, past Saturn. Ahead I see bright galaxies spinning together, spiraling into each other's arms as Lucy and I embrace for the first time in so long a time.

Colliding forever, unconsumed, we give birth to new light. 

Seeds of Power

Seeds of Power

Jerry Craven

Kono followed me to the edge of the village. "Which way?" I asked.

"I'm not sure." He shrugged.

"In that case," I said, "perhaps I ought to get a villager to guide me."

"None of them would help." He turned away from me, seeming to talk to himself. "They love her, but they are afraid of her, the same as I am—the same as any human would be who knew her. She says they aren't human, though, the Salomans, not completely, and maybe she's right. They're all too short, shorter than me, and white as bones, unhealthy white, like Devlin is becoming out there in the caves and with the ironwoods everywhere. These villagers would refuse to take you in the right direction for fear of the caves and the plants that bleed and Devlin herself. If she wanted to be found, she would arrange it, so what I do or do not do isn't an issue, anyway, don't you see?" He turned his palm up in his odd plea for understanding, still facing away from me, seeming to address the jungle. Then he started walking. I followed.

When I asked him what he meant by "the plants that bleed," he ducked his head, alarmed, and muttered to himself.

It was hot and humid, as always on that miserable planet, so whenever I walked much, I sweated. But Kono didn't. I watched him hobble along in his stoop-shouldered gait, arms hanging at his side and occasionally shooting up to punctuate his mumbling. He seemed in many ways more like a malfunctioning machine than a man, and even his madness had a fuzzy, low-key aura about it that became less interesting than annoying.

Several times Kono spoke directly to me. "She is the best agent on the planet," he said. "The best in the galaxy. In the universe. The best. You should hear her talk. Magnificent. Not just what she says, you know, but how she says it, with feeling and understanding. She is a poet and a philosopher, but not one of those who make deductions that sound like cold syllogisms. She speaks with feeling. If you could only hear her!"

I tried to match that assessment with the company agent I knew best, Adrienne Bagg, but to no avail. So far as I could tell, the only thing Bagg wanted more than getting rich from primitive jewelry was to kill Sara Devlin. Oh, she didn't come right out with it, but I could tell that she would put a durden plastic spike into Sara's brain if she ever got close enough to fire a shot. Bagg's motives were hardly obscure: she was openly jealous of Sara's success in getting wealthy from her percentages in the zarlyte she found. If Bagg killed anyone on this planet, chances are she would get away with it. Earth law was light years away.

We trudged on, Kono and I, around clumps of thorns and right through less hostile undergrowth. I sweated; he mumbled. Some of it I understood. "Her temper," he said, eyes wide and arms waving. "Her temper. Rage. Fury, fury. As profound as her eloquence. And her appetite. Like nothing you have ever seen. Appetite for native jewelry, to be sure, but for other things, too, for . . ." He trailed off into incoherence.

And later, while we sat resting against the vast trunk of an ironwood tree: "I love being with her. Even if she can do terrible things to you. Terrible things." He had said that when I first arrived and asked him about Sara. And he was mumbling something similar after we had resumed our trek through the underbrush, just before the Salomans appeared.

It was quite sudden: we seemed alone, then there they were, like so many white specters materializing from the brush, each aiming one of their sword-like river shark spines at us—or, more accurately, at me. I let my hand drift toward my spike pistol at my belt, but Kono stopped me. "They know what that is," he warned, "and you will die if you so much as touch it." I thought of Harold Upson, the expert on primitive modes of travel whom I had replaced in the company. I had found a nevel bush growing up through his skeleton, the river shark's spine that killed him still among the bones. And I left the spike pistol alone.

One Saloman relieved me of my weapon, then pointed the direction he wanted me to walk, urging me along with some quick shakes of his shark spine. They ignored Kono, who dropped into step with them. "Seven of them," he observed to no one in particular. "Seven. The usual number." Then, to me: "Did you notice the scars on their foreheads? Seeds of power make those. This group is hers, all right. Now you will get to meet her for sure. Likely you will be sorry."

I was sorry before I met her. It wasn't the wild Salomans with the dotted lines of scar tissue on their foreheads that bothered me. I knew I was in a bit of a scrape, but it didn't seem so serious to me. It was when we got to the plants that bleed that I regretted being held captive by that bunch. I wanted the leisure to examine them.

The first one we came to wasn't much more than a squat, thick stump with a few underprivileged-looking leaves on it. The leaves were like thin membranes, laced with veins that had that bluish look about them like the veins on your arm. "If you pick one of those, the plant will bleed," Kono informed me as we trooped by the stumpy plant. "Only don't ever do it when these Salomans are around or they are apt to make you bleed, too."

There were others, some that looked much like the smaller plants that normally grew between the massive trunks of the ironwoods, only the texture of the bark and the leaves looked more like woody flesh than a tree has any business doing. And there were ones that were masses of thorns, or maybe horns is a better description. "Some are deadly poison," Kono said, pointing to an orange thing that looked like a cross between a saguaro cactus and an anteater. "That one is a killer." There were bones of small animals all around its base. Several of the plants were exquisitely beautiful, like petrified birds of paradise with roots.

The Salomans took greater care with me when we got into the area where the plants were numerous. They walked on both sides of me, and they made it clear that I should not touch any of the vegetation.

We dropped into a gully that widened into a rather broad arroyo. The ironwood trees seemed not to have taken much notice of the aberrations in the land; they jutted out of the arroyo about ten meters apart, the same as everywhere else on the planet. At the end of the arroyo appeared a gaping black hole, like a rip in the cliff wall.

Sara Devlin stood, arms akimbo, beside the entrance to the cave. Her scant clothing looked freshly laundered, though how she managed that out there in the jungle was a mystery to me. She tilted her head back and looked at us in almost a sneer.

But she was beautiful—in a wild sort of way: beautiful and, I remember thinking, powerful, though I wasn't exactly sure I saw power in her face or imagined it because of what Kono had led me to expect. The Salomans and Kono treated her as if she had plenty of power over them. They were almost disgusting in their fawning body language, like so many lickspittle lesser bureaucrats before a company executive. And she wasn't even armed.

"I'm Balan Clive," I said, trying to act as if I were there on a social call rather than as her captive. I offered my hand, and even took a couple of steps forward, but she kept her hands on her hips.

"Not yet." Without taking her eyes off me, she addressed Kono: "I suppose they packed up my zarlyte, and that you led them to it?"

"Yes," Kono said. "But I stayed out of your home. Adrienne Bagg is keeping records, on account of your percentages. I saw—"

"She might get it, but she won't keep it." Devlin struck her palm with her fist. "I can see to that. It is mine, not even the company's. Mine. The jungle gave it to me, and the caves of power, and I took what was offered. So she wants to take me back, I suppose. As her captive, no doubt. But she won't, not me, not so long as I have the seeds and know how to use them as no one else could." The speech was beyond my understanding. But I did detect a fanatical devotion to the personal pronouns *I*, *me*, and *mine*, that sounded quite unhealthy. Her face flushed, as if she were too hot or had a fever. She had the same scar tissue on her forehead that the Salomans had, only hers was only above one eye. I could see some button-like white spots that the natives didn't have.

Sara turned to me. "Did Bagg send you to take me back?" Her voice mocked.

"No. I came to meet you. I don't give a hang about the green stones or about percentages or company profit."

Exactly why was I there? I wondered. But I might just as well have asked myself why I was on Helios Four at all, or what pushed me to take Paulson jumps into deep space. I was there because of the ironwoods, because they reclaimed landing fields at staggering rates, because fifty meters up their branches matted well enough to stop a shuttle, because the best way to get around on that planet was on internal-combustion-driven boats, because I knew the primitive technology. The ironwoods got me the job, then. But why I had wanted it was another matter, one I truthfully did not know. That itch to get into deep space, to see exotic worlds, maybe. And then it became an itch to see Sara Devlin, whom everyone assured me was a truly remarkable person.

"Everyone wants a profit," she said. "If not in currency, then in something else, something to fill the empty void within. I should know about that. You won't carry off anything material from me. Not here, not from my world. But I might let you learn to fill your nightmares with dreams sweeter than the love of wealth. I might allow that. I might just give you the chance to learn. I'll shake your hand now." She approached me, hand out. Kono and the Salomans shrank from her.

2. *Becoming a Cat*

Her hand felt feverish, and her eyes had that hard white glint people get when their body temperature rises above normal. She kept my hand, and I stood motionless and mute; it took me a few seconds to realize that something profound had taken place inside me, something alarming. The muscles in my body no longer obeyed what I commanded

Becoming a Cat

them to do. I couldn't even look around at Kono for a clue to what was going on. I tried: I willed the action. But my body stayed where it was, my eyes fixed on the woman who held my hand.

"You don't mean to give him the seeds of power?" Kono asked, his voice going almost into a shriek.

Sara laughed. "It is a gift he just might appreciate," she said, then addressed the Salomans in their language, dismissing them. I heard them retreating down the arroyo.

"But he might become one of those plants that bleed—" Kono's voice trailed off into a mumble.

"He might. You go, now, Kono. And you are through serving as a guide. Do you understand my meaning perfectly?"

"Perfectly." Kono sounded defeated.

Devlin walked me into the cave. I don't know how else to describe it: she walked me, literally,assuming control in some mysterious way, moving my limbs. My body became a puppet, she the puppet master.

I could feel the air become cool, was aware of the fever in the hand that held mine, could smell the foreign musk of the cave, but there was nothing, absolutely nothing I could do with all that sensual data. I was along for the ride. When the Salomans had marched me along as their prisoner, I could have chosen to bolt and run for it. But as Devlin's prisoner, free will vanished.

The cave floor slanted downward, and the tunnel took several turns. But it wasn't dark. An eerie green light, electric green or maybe blue, seemed to radiate from the walls, the floor, enough for faint vision. As my eyes adjusted, I could see farther ahead, and found the light bright enough to cast weird shadows among the rubble in the sides of the cave. She

talked as we walked, though at first I felt so disoriented that I heard little. When I regained composure, I found Sara in the midst of an extraordinary monologue, one that told me she was as mad as Kono, but in far more interesting ways: ". . . just a few millimeters thick, but enough. It grows as fast as the ironwoods, and all of the caves of power are aglow with the green fungus. The tribe has great reverence for it, and their first night in the cave is spent in ritual meditation of its light. The second night has to be in the chamber of power, where they drink the juice of the neloc flower before the seeds climb into place and become them into knowledge. It's a rite of passage everyone in the tribe must go through at age twenty-one—or upon attaining the age of seven for the third time, they say, since they have no word for a number above seven. There is wisdom in that, a profound simplicity that keeps them primitive, and they must be primitive in order to have vitality in life."

At that point, my body sat on the floor of the cave and she released my hand, keeping her finger tips close to my face. "You may talk now."

"How are you controlling me? Why—" My voice stopped working when her hot fingers touched my face.

"Don't ask foolish questions," she commanded. When her fingers drew back, I was under my own control again. I searched for a way to get away from her, but there was none. All she had to do was touch me, and I became her slave.

"Did you make the plants that bleed?" I asked.

She laughed, the music of it echoing in the cave. "No. Those are the people who suffer from a loss of nerve. Come on." She took control again, and we walked on. "One night in the chamber of power is enough for the Salomans, and there they learn all that they need to know to be more alive than any of us with our books and machines. But they lack the linear mental constructs to even consider using the seeds as I have done. It is I who have learned to synthesize, to bring the greatest of two cultures together, to transcend self as they do and at the same time to assert self ultimately and finally as we strain to do but cannot. Some die. Not an actual death, for you saw them, the plants that bleed, as the Salomans call them. With the seeds of power upon them, they look at life with all its power and vitality. Some see only the horror and the pain, so they grow themselves into forms that escape it all. With the seeds, you can do anything." Her words were growing weak and breathy. She stopped us and stood beside me, breathing in short, shallow gulps. "I'm afraid you will have to carry me." She moved my body around to pick her up, placing one of my arms under her knees, the other supporting her back. I wanted to speak again, but there was no hope for that. And after carrying her some distance, my muscles cried out for rest. It wasn't a cry I could vocalize, nor did she think to give me a rest.

"With the seeds, you get exactly what you want from life," she whispered, her lips puffing the air right into my ear.

I walked on, formulating questions for when she next released me. What were the seeds? How did the Salomans grow into plants? Would I be forced to metamorphose in such a horrible way?

She sighed, pressing her feverish cheek against my neck. Inside I recoiled from her touch, but only inside. "The ones who want to live but cannot bear the suffering, the cowards, wander out in the night and root themselves in the soil. Any of us could do that, if we could find the keys to the cells so we could unlock them and rebuild. The ones who chose unconscious life after the rite of passage are fools. To avoid pain, they give up all possibility of ecstasy. Can you imagine giving up desire? For sleep, for unknowing physical functions. But that's what some people want, I guess. Those who restrain desire do so because theirs is weak enough to be restrained, and they surely kept a lid on desire even before coming to the caves. They come here to seal that lid. Of course, they don't know that, so they come here in terror of the very condition that they have chosen and will choose after the seeds drop away, leaving them with knowledge they need to become plants. Fools!"

She walked me on in silence until the descent flattened and we passed smaller tunnels branching elsewhere. Jagged teeth of stalactites and stalagmites appeared here and there, ominous in the green light. Then we stepped into the chamber.

It was huge, echoing, beyond my ability to measure with sight. She walked me to a small pond that had water dripping in slow rhythm from a gigantic stalactite. She had me set her down, then laid me on what felt like a fur carpet beside the pool. She put me on my back, knelt beside the pool, and reached toward the water. "You won't have my power, not power over others, but you might gain something. If you have the courage to be alive. It will happen mainly inside. Remember that: you will be inside, but you must make an effort to stay outside. Only after several times did I learn how to wear half of the seeds and gain power." I could hear her hand splashing in the pool, feeling around for something. Her other hand she kept on my cheek.

"On the second night the Salomans come here, drug themselves, and sleep. Then this crawls from the water." She held what looked like a string of beads above my face, dripping water upon me. I began to feel the churn of terror in my gut, but there was nothing I could do about it. The beads writhed, and I could see that each bead had two pointed feet or claws, like those of a centipede. "I know this is frightening, but you will learn to thank me. If you choose to live." She laid the beads on my forehead, and I felt the wetness of them, then a stinging as they settled upon me.

Sun warmed the rock and my fur, and it felt good to want nothing—not food or water—but merely to sit and watch the beaver in the pond below me. I liked the way it pushed logs about. A vague memory of the cave and Devlin danced around my consciousness, but it was not something I could understand. I knew understanding was beyond me because I was merely a cat, and at that moment all I wanted was to watch the beaver. From my right came a slight gleam of metal and glass, but I knew it was not something that would harm me, so I ignored it, concentrating on the graceful swimming of the beaver.

It was easy to sweep back and see the cat that was me, and the photographer who was feeling so fortunate as to have found such a magnificent cat to photograph. I knew the feeling, because I was the photographer looking through the lens. It had taken much trouble to climb the steep hill across the beaver pond, and it was something of a pain to sit so still for so long, but the waiting paid off when the mountain lion came to watch the beaver.

"Come outside," Sara Devlin said. The beaver, the cat, the camera lens vanished, and I found myself in the cave with Devlin.

"You drugged me."

She shook her head, but I knew she was about to lie to me. "It's the seeds of power." She grinned a wicked, lying grin. "I thought it was a drug at first, but it's not. It's a symbiotic animal that awakens our own powers. The Salomans always go inward. I did that, but with only half of the seeds, I stay outside. Mostly." She smiled at me, and the smile became a leer, evil and toothy.

Flesh began to drip from her face like so much wax melting away from the bone. The grin remained a constant, and I could easily perceive its deceptive intent by the expressionless eye sockets and the dark shadows of the cheek bones. She was Yorick, long dead, speaking through the death's head. She was Dorian Gray and Mr. Hyde.

"I thought if I gave you a full segment, you might go inside, as I did, but that I could get you to focus on the outside. This might help." It was hideous to hear calm words coming from the stark skull. She shifted her gown and pulled it off over her head. The melted flesh reassembled into her original features. It happened fast—just in the few seconds it took to lift the gown over her head. The green light brightened into a glow focusing on her breasts.

Devlin stood before me and beside a wonderful elephant while a part of me wondered if the planet supported elephants though the answer was clear as the net clothing Sara Devlin wore: there are no elephants within many lightyears of this planet where she stood, where I stood as a mandrake watching her.

I felt cool, comfortable, natural, and rooted in the earth with both legs. I lived in medieval England, so there was danger in being a mandrake. In the spring an apothecary might stumble across me while he was out simpling, so I could be uprooted, and I would scream when my roots were jerked from the soil.

Fish swam by, and a galaxy of sea life, perch, blowfish, oysters. The oyster was the best, for I could peer out of my shell by opening it only a tiny crack and watch fish, eel, shrimp, crabs, sea grasses whirl in their dance of celebration of life. I could see it well enough through the crack, but if I dared open even more, perhaps the scene would become a panorama of life, of creatures moving, interesting. I dared push the doors of my shell apart more, straining to see.

"I want to help you with the initial difficult time, if I can," Sara said. She was beautiful, wrapped in soft shades of green, a perfect Picasso nursing a child, the Madonna, her eyelids swept down, head inclined better to see the beauty of the child at her breast. She wore a green halo. She was the giver of life, and I the child nursing.

"Did you slip inside again?" The light in the room burned. "Try reaching out." She looked down at her breasts, inhaling and leaning toward me in an invitation to touch. The light in the room warmed crimson, a harsh, uncomfortable color that carried too much heat. I broke into a sweat.

In the brighter light, I could see that it wasn't a child that she held at all, but her rumpled gown. And the halo had been a trick of the shadows that had drawn my attention away from the tiny horns just visible in her hair. "Move back," I said. "Even your name suggests the demonic."

But that is silly, I told myself; the universe operates without gods and devils. The universe is . . . I searched for a metaphor and found it in the lens of the camera. I was the lens all along, even when I thought I was the cat and then the photographer. I was the lens looking at the cat through the large end and back at the tiny eye of the photographer through the small end.

The eye was less interesting. The *I* is always less interesting. So I looked at the cat and made a still-life that could have held forever.

For hours I watched the cat that watched the beaver; I looked from the safety of the metal lens that made up my body.

Or it seemed hours. I awoke from the vision when something slipped from my forehead, slithered across my cheek, rattled some stones, then splashed into the pool.

I sat up on the animal skin where Sara Devlin had put me and looked at the woman lying beside me. Even in the dim light, I could tell her eyes were feverish. "You chose to survive," she said, her voice weak.

She tried to say something else, but lacked the control; her eyes rolled and consciousness faded into the fever. I looked around the cave, feeling a faint stir of anger at her for forcing me into the place. My impulse was to leave her there, to walk out. She evidently had some disease, likely an infection of microbes from the water in the cave, borne by the claws of the creature she wore on one side of her forehead. I felt tempted to let that be punishment for her treatment of me—to leave her there, possibly to die. After all, what had I to do with her being there?

But the seeds of power had told me something about myself, something I didn't like. I was little better than the Salomans who chose to be plants. I was indeed the curious cat, the oyster peering from inside a shell, the camera lens that found the *I* less interesting and was content to watch the world, uninvolved, uncommitted. What was it to me that people around me struggled with envy and avarice, like Adrienne Bagg, with love and hate and madness, like Kono, with vast desire, like Sara? Interesting. That's what it was: interesting. The whirl of human passions that I moved through did not touch me, and my response had always been like my response to the plants that bleed. I simply wanted to look at my leisure, to satisfy my curiosity.

Sitting there in the strange green light of the caves of power, I looked at what I had been, and found it lacking: I did not like being a camera lens.

The button-like beads on the right side of Sara's forehead came loose when I pulled on one with steady pressure. I tossed them back into the black waters. Sara stirred, mumbling in a fevered sleep. I started to pick her up, then realized with a start that her breasts were bare.

It shouldn't have mattered what she wore or didn't wear, not then when I was needed to carry her out of there so she could get medical help. I knew it shouldn't have mattered.

But it did, and even as I struggled without success to put the gown on her, I knew what the crimson light and the horns had meant. At that moment the effort to dress her didn't seem to matter so much. I threw her gown into the pool, swallowed hard in trying to set aside my fears, and picked her up. Sara Devlin was beautiful, so beautiful it made me catch my breath. And while part of me, an older part that seemed to be slipping into the past, feared the intimate contact of her flesh against mine, a newer part of me liked the touching.

But I resolved to deal with all that sort of thing later. Right then it felt good to lift her fevered body and move out of that dark cave toward daylight. It felt good to know I could join the dance of the eel, shrimp, and sea grasses, that I could move from the lens into the whirl of human passions, even with the full awareness that the soft green halo could well be worn by one with horns.

That time when I carried her, I didn't tire. At the entrance of the cave, I set Sara on the ground and rubbed my shoulder. "Clive?" Kono's voice sounded panicked. I looked around but could not locate him. "Is she, uh, is she dead?"

"Not yet. And I will not let her die."

Kono emerged from behind a rock, glancing around with fear. "Her Salomans are nearby. They'll kill us if they see her like this and us beside her." He knelt by her and put a hand on her forehead. "They die when they get like this, some of them. Other Salomans put down roots, and become plants that bleed."

"She won't become a plant—no more than I could ever again become a mandrake." I picked her up. "She's alive. And so am I, maybe for the first time in my life. Lead us back to the camp."

"You can't carry her that far." Kono's voice took on a shrill edge.

"It will be difficult." I spoke to him in a soothing tone. "But I must do it. Kono, I will never again watch people with the idleness of a cat or choose to be the lens of a camera or the oyster."

"You say such lucid things." Kono clasped his hands as in ecstasy. "You've become like Sara Devlin—so magnificent." I liked carrying Sara, liked pressing the warmth of her against me there in the heat of the ironwood jungle and the fire of commitment. I liked it that a madman thought me lucid and eloquent.

It was a good way to begin the journey.

Space Migration

Space Migration

Terry Dalrymple

Cassie, our cute little bush pilot, turned from her controls, glanced back at Shayla and me, and said, "I can take you there if you like. But it's, you know, pricey."

Shayla hates that I refer to the excursion guide as "our cute little bush pilot," but that's what she was. Cute. Damn cute and also little. She was five-two or -three, with small feet, small hands, and a small nose perfect for her pixie face. And she had been an Alaskan bush pilot before getting into the float plane excursion business, now hauling cruise people like us on tours of glaciers near Juneau. And, at least for that one afternoon, she was ours, our pilot exclusively because her plane only accommodated her and two passengers. So she really was "our cute little bush pilot."

She was having us on, I knew, but I played along. "How pricey?"

She glanced in a mirror positioned for seeing her passengers, told me the price, and flashed a bright smile directly at me. I bugged my eyes at Shayla and winked. "Any chance of a discount for special passengers?" Shayla rolled her eyes.

Cassie said, "Maybe. Depends on how special." Again she flashed the pixie smile.

"Oh," I said, "very, very special." Shayla scowled, so I dropped my flirtatious posturing.

Shayla and I had booked an Alaskan cruise for our twenty-fifth anniversary and had decided on the float-plane excursion for the Juneau stopover. Rising toward the glacier, Cassie had told us about her bush pilot days delivering medical supplies to otherwise inaccessible communities of indigenous people. And then she dropped the explosive claim that once, leaving an especially remote community

in a blizzard, she had flown nearly straight up to rise above the storm and crossed into outer space before escaping it. There, she said, she followed a flock of space pelicans that led her hundreds of miles through the cosmos before pointing their beaks at a safe place to exit. Eventually, she explained, she landed in a South American desert, the Patagonian, she thought.

"So," I teased, "space pelicans flew hundreds of miles just to save you."

She shrugged. "Well, I think so, but maybe they were migrating anyway."

"Oh, yes, space migration. I think I've heard of that."

"Anyway," she said, "I can take you there. You know, to outer space. But it's pricey."

After our flirtatious dickering, I said, "Let's go—as long as we can get that extra special discount." Shayla scowled more severely. I knew I should back off, but I couldn't resist calling our cute little bush pilot's bluff.

Cassie giggled and flashed me a precious smile and pulled the plane into ascent. I watched the altimeter, sure that she would fly some loop-de-loops that would dizzy us enough that when she said so we'd believe we had been to outer space. But she didn't fly loop-de-loops. She flew almost straight up, 12,000, 13,000, 14,000 feet. At 15,000, my palms began to sweat.

Shayla glared at me and silently mouthed, "Asshole."

The plane shook and rattled, so I yelled to be heard. "I thought these planes topped out at twelve or thirteen thousand feet."

Cassie giggle again. "Not this baby. But

not to worry. She's pressurized and oxygenated."

Shayla, pale and visibly trembling, slugged my arm and hissed, "Tell her to stop."

I chuckled, though I'll admit I did so unsurely. "She'll reverse course soon."

When we hit 30,000 feet, I began to doubt myself. This little firecracker of a bush pilot was either confident or crazy.

I clutched Shayla's hand, and she seemed thankful to have something to squeeze. "I'm going to divorce you," she said between clenched teeth. "And then I'm going to kill you."

I was pretty sure she meant it, but I closed my eyes and prayed it was just an expression. I either slept or blacked out, because the next time our surroundings were familiar again we were at 100,000 feet. Three times that much, maybe a little more, we'd cross that magical line.

"Cassie." I screamed to be heard. "We changed our minds. Take us down." She flashed a pixie grin in the mirror, though by then it seemed to me more Satanic than pixie-ish.

"Okay," she said. "But it'll still cost you."

"Fine. Just take us down."

Back on the ground, legs shaking, Shayla knocked that damn cute smile off Cassie's face, and a tooth went with it.

When Shayla stormed off, I offered Cassie a sheepish grin. "Sorry," I said. "I still love ya."

She spat blood on my shoes and made an unnatural, unearthly hissing noise. I slunk away.

Shayla did not divorce me, nor did she kill me, but now she spends her nights in ratty flannel pajamas with her back to me. She needs space, she says. I think I need space too. Once Shayla sleeps, I spend my nights at the window, gazing at the stars and wondering if Cassie could have done it and regretting that I'll never know. But I've been considering moving to Juneau for the summer. A little space migration might do me good. mMm

The general's wife went bubbling slack down into the China Sea . . .
Jerry Craven

A Strange Painting

Castle Moon

Terry Dalrymple

Andrew Geyer

Jerry Craven

1. *A Strange Painting*

As was his habit, Robert walked to the local grocery six blocks from his modest pier-and-beam house. The chilly morning air invigorated him, and he felt happy to be outside under a cloudless sky and bright winter sun. On his way past Eddie's store, Genuine Texas, he glanced in the front window and spotted a painting he had never seen before, an odd painting that depicted a castle, a night sky full of stars, clearly visible planets, and a large gray cloud from which tentacled lightning flashed above a large body of water. A bit lurid, Robert thought, but somehow interesting, the more so because Eddie had never carried anything like it.

Robert walked on toward the grocery store but couldn't quite get the painting out of his head. Though it did not fit his typical taste in art, there was something about it, something in it that a brief look could not absorb.

The grocery store, Catclaw Market, named after the small Texas town it served, was owned by Bill and Anna Schwartz, who were known for carrying beautifully marbled beef, an impressive variety of frozen seafood, and crisp fresh vegetables. No one quite knew how such a small business managed to offer such fine comestibles, but everyone certainly appreciated it. Robert selected hanger steak and several salad greens, as well as a few staples for his pantry.

Strolling home with his arms wrapped around paper grocery bags, Robert paused again in front of Genuine Texas. Eddie claimed to sell fine Texas art, jewelry, and decor, which everyone knew was made in Mexico or China or was just some old crap Eddie found along the road or on somebody's ranch. He was a nice guy, a good friend, but he was lazy and got by doing the easiest thing he could to make a few bucks. The painting was dim because it sported a thick layer of dust. Robert entered to take a closer look.

Eddie was nowhere in sight, probably snoozing in the storeroom chair. The painting, once Robert dusted it off, fascinated him even more. A planet that looked suspiciously like Earth loomed behind the castle, suggesting that the castle was elsewhere in the universe. But there was something other than the ominous science fiction feel to it, something in several formless shapes that hinted at form and seemed important. Robert called Eddie's name and after a pause called louder. Eddie ambled out of the back room, yawning and rubbing his eyes.

Robert held up the painting. "How much?"

Eddie squinted. "Fifty."

"No way. I'll give you five."

Eddie shrugged. "Okay." Then he chuckled. "I got it for free some years back. Stuck it in the storeroom and forgot it until I ran across it yesterday."

"Where'd you get it?"

Eddie frowned. Thinking often seemed to be hard for him. Finally he said, "I think it was the old Weishuhn place. You know, when they sold the ranch and had that auction for pretty much everything else." He shook his head. "Hated to see them go. They were good folks."

Robert's nod was grim. "The best," he said.

"Anyway, that painting was in a bin of free stuff."

"Something's interesting about it," Robert said. "Come by this evening and help me figure out what it is."

"You fixing supper?"

Robert rolled his eyes. "Okay, I'll feed you. I'll invite Dale, too."

"You're on."

Eddie had always been a freeloader. Dale took care of himself, but they both raved about Robert's cooking, even when he prepared something they'd never heard of. The three of them were an unlikely trio, but they had been fast friends since they met at school, Catclaw Elementary.

After high school, they all attended Tarleton State University, but only Robert completed a degree. Eddie, smart enough but just too lazy, flunked out after his freshman year. Robert tried graduate school down at Lamar U, but soon dropped out after spending most of his time in the Angelina Forest farther north, enjoying small-town Jasper and hiking along Muddy Creek, examining trees and bushes. Dale got through his sophomore year and then quit because he was an ace mechanic and didn't need a degree to open a garage of his own. He made an excellent living for his family; but as soon as they could, his two sons moved to larger towns. Dale had been widowed within the last six months and had just recently retired.

Eddie barely scraped by, and his wife eventually took the kids and headed for greener pastures. Real estate sales were infrequent for Robert simply because of the area in which he worked, but when that occasional large family ranch sold, the payoff was large enough for him to live a pleasant, moderate life. He too had recently retired. He had never married. Dale and Eddie wondered if he might be gay, but they never asked and he never volunteered such information. With two of them retired and one barely working except to open his store every weekday and nap in the storeroom, they spent more time together than ever.

Eddie entered Robert's house a little after three and found his friend hunched over the painting in the kitchen. Robert clutched a mug of coffee in his left hand and a pencil in the other. On the front edge of table lay a hand-written note and next to it a blank note pad. The painting was just behind them.

"Clues?"

"Eddie, who painted this?"

"Beats me. It's not signed."

"I noticed. But I found this note taped to the back of it. Listen to this:

*Please find what must be found in the
small town that produced me.
An alien raccoon above an odd moon
Sees a starfish already dead
while a redfish nearby in a dark bit of sky
Sees a shark not far up ahead.
One other clue in this strange cosmic stew
Is a sibilant staff by a bed.*

Eddie frowned. "Damned mysterious."

"We have to figure this out."

"I don't know," Eddie said. "Sounds time-consuming."

"What the hell else do we have to do these days?"

"I have the store."

"Where you nap."

Eddie shrugged, then smiled. "True enough." They both peered at the painting.

Dale arrived at five, and the other two caught him up on the mystery. "I'm in," Dale said. He opened a bag he had brought with him and pulled out a six-pack of Shiner. "Anyone for a beer?"

They hunched over the painting, which they had named "Castle Moon" because the two areas seemed to draw the eye first: the castle in the lower left and the large moon in the upper right above the lightning. After tilting his bottle back to get the last sip of beer, Dale pointed to a brownish shape on top of a mountain and below the gray cloud. "There," he said. "That's the raccoon." He slammed his empty bottle down, obviously proud of his find.

"Damn," Robert said, "you're right."

Eddie looked, squinted, frowned. "I'll be go to hell," he marveled.

Robert announced that he'd fix dinner but that Dale and Eddie should keep looking. Instead, Eddie followed him to the kitchen. "Got any snacks?"

Robert pointed to a jar of unsalted, dry-roasted peanuts. "Help yourself." His friend, he knew, preferred the greasy, salty variety but didn't hesitate to pour out a handful of the healthier option. Dale soon joined them, offering another round of Shiner. Robert cooked and the others asked questions. What is that? What are you doing? Why are you doing it that way? How'd you learn all this? Neither would remember Robert's patient answers, and even if they did they'd never try it out themselves. And in truth, the meal was simple, just some medium rare hanger steak cubes over a bed of spinach, kale, and mushroom slices. When the meal was served, Eddie and Dale groaned with pleasure every time they took a bite. Robert smiled.

After the meal, Dale's beer gone, they switched to Robert's Rebecca Creek blended whiskey, which Eddie was too broke to buy and Dale too frugal. They all preferred on the rocks.

By 2:00 a.m. they were sure they had found all of the vague shapes: raccoon, redfish, starfish, shark, sibilant staff, and bed. And, of course, the much more obvious odd moon. But except for the fish, they could make out no relationship among the images.

"We're going to have to scour this town for answers," Robert said.

Dale agreed. "I'm in."

"Sounds like a lot of work," Eddie said.

The other two rolled their eyes.

2. *New Love*

Special. Ophelia Weishuhn was special. How many times had her father told her so? Every day, it seemed, of her sixteen years and two days of life. But it was only two days ago, on her sixteenth birthday, that he'd explained to her precisely why and how.

And now, after 48 ½ hours locked in her bedroom alternately sobbing out her window at the low rolling hills of cactus and mesquite, reading from the sheaf of papers that her father had given her to "document" his explanation, and sleeping from exhaustion caused by both her reading and her tears, she had come to a realization:

She would give anything in the world to be ordinary.

Just plain old ordinary everyday. And for the world to go back to the way it had been only forty-nine hours ago. Forty-nine hours. It seemed like a lifetime now.

Time. What did it even matter anymore after what her father had told her?

And life? Why would she want it to go on?

New Love

And on? And on?

"Mendel's Law of Segregation," her father had said, "is elegant in its ruthlessness." This was in response to a question from Ophelia about the article he'd shared with her the day before "The Talk." The article concerned a jellyfish called *Turritopsis dohrnii*—a species that, her father said, "has come to be known as 'the immortal jellyfish'. And in every way that matters," he continued, "you are that jellyfish. We are. You and me, and your mother before she passed. And we were not, are not, alone."

Her father, an MD, went on to explain—calmly, evenly—in his best bedside-manner voice, exactly what that meant. "We call ourselves *Evergreen*. Although we are not immortal, we do not age. A genetic mutation keeps our telomeres from degrading. We can be killed. And far too many of us have been killed —your mother among them—but we cannot die of disease. As is the case with *Turritopsis dohrnii*, a process called transdifferentiation makes us immune. By undergoing transdifferentiation," he continued, "an adult cell that is specialized for a particular tissue becomes an entirely different type of specialized cell. It's an efficient way of cell recycling, and an important area of study in cutting-edge stem cell research among those who are merely human. But unlike *Turritopsis dohrnii*," he pointed at the photo of the jellyfish, a delicate and lovely mix of gossamer and bright red, "we Evergreens don't produce offspring that are genetically identical to ourselves. And therein lies our tragedy."

"What tragedy?" Ophelia asked, feeling a little sick.

"The one that Mendel describes so elegantly in his most ruthless genetic law: segregation. Not all of our descendants have the pure mutation, you see. Only a quarter of newborns (on average) are fully Evergreen. Half are longer-lived than the unmutated human species. A quarter are merely human. And so the cost of our potentially infinite long life is watching three-quarters of our children grow old and die."

"Okay, so you're Evergreen. And Mom was. But if only a quarter of newborns have the pure mutation, how do you know that 25% includes me?"

"Because of the genetic test your mother and I did the day after you were born."

"Dad . . . what if . . . what if I don't want to be Evergreen?"

"Don't be foolish, Ophie. No one wants to grow old and die."

But Ophelia wasn't so sure of that. Particularly not after he'd gone on to explain the implications of what being "pure" meant for her sixteen-year-old, secretly deeply-in-love self.

"There are reasons why we separate ourselves from those who are unlike us. Aside from the very real threat of their xenophobia, when we reproduce with mere humans, the percentage of newborns with the pure mutation is even worse. We must be very careful, you see, about whom we choose as mates. You must swear to me, Ophelia, that you will only date, and eventually marry, one of our own kind—one who is fully Evergreen—and that you will never reveal what I have told you to any mere human . . ."

But all of that only half-explained why Ophelia Weishuhn sat staring out the window at the low rolling West Texas hills and sobbing into the coming sunset. The other half of the equation was Robert McCaskill, the "mere human" who was almost certainly waiting for her out there in the brush.

Like her father, Robert had also told

Ophelia that she was special—but for a very different reason. Robert was in love with her. He loved her even more, he said, than the semi-desert land and plants that he'd shown her the magic of.

At just seventeen years old, Robert already knew the secrets of that spare, arid, gorgeous West Texas country of cactus and mesquite that Ophelia saw every time she looked out her window. And he had shared those secrets with her, ever since that May day six months ago when they met in a clearing not far from the Colorado River. Ophelia was out wandering, as she often did when she got tired of studying. Her father insisted on home-schooling her; and her lessons, although fascinating, were lonely indeed. So she'd been intrigued, rather than afraid, when she came across a boy—actually a young man, she realized—standing next to a thicket of bushes that had deep green spiny leaves with clusters of red berries interspersed inside them. He'd spread a blanket on the ground underneath the bushes, and was whacking the limbs with what looked like a broom handle. Every time the stick connected with the spiny-leaved branches, more of the red berries dropped into the waiting blanket.

The young man himself was at least as intriguing as the process he was engaged in. His hair was so blonde as to be almost white, his body darkly tanned and wiry. And he was blue-eyed, she saw, as he sensed her presence and turned to face her.

"Agaritas," he said, apparently reading in her expression the question she had not yet voiced. He smiled, picked up a handful of bright red berries. "The stick is the best way to harvest them because of the spines on the leaves." He popped a few of the berries into his mouth and then reached the rest in her direc-tion.

She approached, encouraged by his lop-sided smile, and held out her hand. He filled it with the bright red berries. They were about a quarter-inch in diameter. When she imitated his movement, popping a few of the berries into her mouth, they had a sweet, slightly acidic flavor.

"Delicious," she said.

"Birds love them too," he said. "And they're great for making jelly and wine." Then his smile widened and she saw that his teeth were stained red. "I'm Robert."

"Ophelia." She found herself grinning back and wondering if her teeth were as red as his.

It was the beginning of what had grown into the great love of her young life. The only love, really. Day after day they wandered the West Texas countryside together. He knew all about the plants they walked among: which varieties could be used for food and which for medicine, and which should not be touched. And he shared it with her—not the way her father did, with books and magazines and aca-demic papers, but hands-on. Every time they met, he brought her something new to taste and then showed her how to forage it. He told her tales of the first peoples—Tonkawas, Wichitas, Comanches, and Lipan Apaches—who had foraged the land for centuries; and of the White settlers who came and foraged the land after them, all the way up to the time of supply chains and supermarkets.

But even more than the things he taught her, the young man was himself a revelation. Ophelia wasn't allowed to date yet. She wasn't even allowed to be alone with boys, except her cousins and a select group her father approved. She didn't much like the boys he introduced her to at the gatherings they sometimes traveled to. In fact, she didn't much like any of those people. And she'd begun to wonder if they might not be part of a cult.

But Robert was nothing like those boys. "Exotic," he called her, one day in June, and "lovely." It was the week before the Summer Solstice. "Like a Wichita princess," he said, then he leaned in and kissed her.

The magic of that first kiss was like nothing she'd felt before.

Then came Midsummer's Day, when he fed her dewberries along the bank of the Colorado River, showing her how to pluck the wild blackberries from their low, trailing vines. "You can identify the plant," Robert said, "by its thorny stems and white, five-petaled flowers. The berries start out green, then turn red, but are sweetest when they're deep black and fully ripe. Like your eyes."

After a long time of kissing, they went skinny-dipping in the Colorado. Afterward, on Robert's berry blanket, they did what comes naturally to fifteen- and seventeen-year-olds who are wildly in love. Since then, on most of the days she couldn't go out wandering, she'd been slipping out to meet him at night. The last time she'd seen him, three days before "The Talk," he promised her a gift for her sixteenth birthday. "A special surprise," he said, "for your sweet sixteen." But then came her father's revelation, the accompanying explanation, the packet of documentation, the promises she'd made. And now? Now they were leaving, her father had said. Moving away, three days from today. For a place called Monastir, on the coast of Tunisia, where her father owned a home on a cliff overlooking the Mediterranean Sea. One of the things he'd made her promise was that she wouldn't leave the house.

And that was why she was staring out the window now, waiting for Robert.

As the sun finally sank bloodred behind the West Texas hills, there came a noise outside her bedroom window, a scrapy-scratchy sound like the whisper of mesquite branches across a tin roof. It came again, and yet again. She opened the window a crack, then a couple more inches, and through the gap between the window and the sill came the bare thread of a whisper.

"I came looking for a Wichita princess."

"Robert!" she half-whispered, half-sobbed. Too loud, she knew, but she couldn't help herself. "What are you doing here?"

"Shh! I came to ask you that same question. What's kept you? Don't you . . . don't you love me anymore?"

"Of course I love you." She opened the window wide and pressed her face against the screen. "I'll always love you. But th—"

"But nothing. The only thing that matters is that we love each other. And of course, the fact that I brought you a birthday present. Can you slip out?"

"Listen to me. There's something . . . secret, about me and about my family, that my father made me swear not to tell. Something that you need to know."

"It'll be okay, I promise. We'll be okay. No matter what. Just please come out."

"Alright. I'm coming. Help me with the screen!"

As he pulled the bottom of the screen away from the window sill, Robert handed something through. "Here. Take this while I lift the screen off the hinge clips."

What Ophelia held in her hand looked like a deer antler, but with intricate whorls and curlicues engraved on the tines and a soft leather cord tightly wrapped about the base to make a handle. "It's lovely. What is it?"

"A talking stick. In Native American tradition when a council was called, a talking stick was passed from person to person in turn. Only the person holding the stick was allowed to speak. You've told me more than once that I'm all the time talking. I figured this might help you get a word in every once in a while. Happy sweet sixteen."

Robert separated the screen from the window sill, finally, then he leaned in and kissed her. For a long moment, everything was right with the world again—and in the whole universe there were only the two of them, in love.

Then the bedroom door burst open, the overhead light flashed on, and her father was in the room. "Ophie! I heard voices. Are you okay? What the hell is going on?"

And Robert was suddenly gone from the window—from the yard, from her line of sight—and things were worse than they had ever been. Instead of angry, her father was heartbroken. They sat on the floor next to her bedroom window together and sobbed. Father and daughter, inconsolable for their own reasons, but united in grief.

"Since I lost your mother," he said, "after a longer time together than you can possibly conceive, there has only been you. You're all I have left, Ophie. What would I do if I lost you? How could I keep on?"

"Why bother living, you mean," Ophelia said slowly, "when there's nothing to live for?"

How could Ophelia do otherwise than pack up and move with her father? But she had no intention of leaving without letting Robert know. Her father had said it would take three days to put the ranch and the house up for sale.

In the meantime, he set her to packing her mother's paintings up for the move. Her mother, Viola, had been a painter, and

Ophelia's most vivid memories of that delicate and lovely lady were of her teaching Ophelia's then-four-year-old self to hold a brush and daub paint on canvas. After her mother's death, Ophelia's father had taken all her paintings down and stacked them against the walls of Viola's study. Ophelia's favorite of them all was the one showing an odd moon and a castle.

That was the one she would leave for Robert.

While her father was out making arrangements for the sale of the ranch and the house, Ophelia was hiding bits of "documentation" from the explanatory packet he'd given her after "The Talk" in one of the places where she and Robert used to wander together—and daubing clues into the "Castle Moon" painting that she hoped would tell Robert where to find them.

In addition to the series of clues in her mother's painting, and the packets that would tell Robert the truth, Ophelia wrote a final love letter that gave details about the house on the cliff in Monastir and invited him to come there. Then she wrote a cryptic poem, a message that would tell him where to begin his journey, and taped it to the back of the painting.

The sibilant staff mentioned in the poem was, of course, the talking stick he'd given her for her birthday. And inside the handle, she'd hidden the letter that would lead him back to her.

3. *Tree Saves Tree*

Images from Robert's long ago walks along the river on the Weishuhn ranch kept coming to him, good memories somehow associated with the painting "Castle Moon," and he felt he was almost remembering something important. The memories were

Tree Saves Tree

vague and indistinct like the voices of trees. Maybe, he thought, having his friends around would help him remember and understand, so he invited Dale and Eddie for drinks and a few light snacks. It came as no surprise to him that they arrived early and hungry. They drank a 6-pack of Shiner, and Robert prepared chicken curry.

After dinner he opened a bottle of Grand-father Rare Tawny Port. He had a feeling about a connection between that odd poem attached to the painting and the river, a good feeling, so good that he decided to share the special port. Dale and Eddie eyed the bottle with delight, especially Eddie.

"Something is up," Eddie said. "You're uncorking the good stuff."

"Are we celebrating something?" Dale asked. "And if so, after we drink this good port, maybe Robert will finally tell us the big thing he can do, like make dust storms stop or predict winners of elections."

"I'll tell you someday," Robert said. "You know that. But not yet." It had been several years since Dale or Eddie had asked, and Robert was pleased with them for not pushing him about the matter.

He knew Dale had some sort of peppery fire inside the first time he saw the boy. He seemed to have some kind of odd aura about him. That was way back in the first grade at Catclaw Elementary, and he could tell Dale saw something about him, too. Most kids sensed something unusual about both of them without understanding anything except that Robert and Dale were weird and needed to be avoided or bullied. But he and Dale were immediately delighted with each other.

When Eddie's family moved to Catclaw, Eddie showed up in their second grade class-room. The new boy ducked his head, made eye contact with nobody until during recess when Robert gave Eddie's arm a shake and the boy looked up, alarm on his face.

"I'm Robert, and this is Dale."

The alarm vanished, replaced by a broad smile, and Robert and Dale knew they had another friend, another with a wild heat inside and an ineffable aura that seemed to be in motion around him.

Of course the bullies showed up to gape without seeing, and the girls showed up to whisper about how they would avoid weird Eddie, as they avoided Dale and Robert.

Within a week Roy Jenkins, the worst and largest bully, began shoving Eddie around on the school ground, something Eddie said he expected. Robert said they didn't have to put up with that crap, and Dale and Eddie agreed, so during recess the three of them tripped Roy and dragged him into a patch of goat-headed grass stickers. They stood over him while Robert explained that if the bullying continued the three of them would do much worse to Roy, not bothering to be specific about the matter.

"He'll imagine us doing meaner things than we would ever dream up," Robert said. The bullying slowed from Roy and everyone else.

But school kids doubled down on Eddie and Dale when they started experimenting.

Dale made it rain in his yard. In a dry year when not a single lawn in town had any green grass and Dale's parents complained about the drought, Dale sat in a swing his father had hung from a live oak branch and watched on the horizon a huge cloud, the kind his parents told Dale was too puffy and white ever to produce rain. He held his hand out, flexing his fingers as if grabbing the cloud, and he felt the power surge through his arm and hand. He watched the cloud move toward him as he compressed it into a dark lump, and he used his other hand in an attempt to grab it and wring the water from it, though it was too far away for him to reach. When it floated overhead, the lumpy black cloud fired a couple of lightning bolts and released itself as large, heavy drops that drenched Dale's yard. People in town expressed astonishment at how the rain came so suddenly and fell in only one yard, and the school kids talked about how that rain was a sign of something bad about weird Dale and his family.

"I made the cloud do that," Dale told his buddies.

Robert nodded, and Eddie said, "Yeah, all of us know."

"None of us should tell anyone or we'll be in trouble," Robert said.

"Not all of us because you two can't make rain," Dale said.

"Not rain, anyway," Eddie said. The two turned to Robert and asked what he could do, and as usual Robert wouldn't say.

They each had a substantial glass of the Grandfather Rare Port while Eddie and Dale thanked Robert profusely. Eddie finished the rest of the bottle, something the other two knew he would do. Robert said, "Okay, guys, we need to get back to the puzzle about the starfsh and shark and maybe think about the Weishuhn ranch. Eddie and Dale stared, clearly flabbergasted. "Okay then," Robert said, "maybe the odd castle moon rhyme had to do with the river that crossed the ranch."

"That makes no sense to me," Dale said.

Eddie was no help. "Sorry guys," he said, "but that port did a number on me."

"It is only twenty percent alcohol," Robert said.

"You call twenty percent *only*?" Dale asked.

Eddie had done too much talking to others when they were in junior high, talking that caused the other kids to start in on him again for being so weird. He flirted with Roy Jenkins's girl, and when she turned away in a huff, he called after her, "Yeah, so your cat will die on Thursday at exactly nine seventeen in the morning."

Judy whirled around. "Are you threatening to harm my Sallie Calley?"

"I won't do a thing. Blunt force trauma will get her. A truck, maybe, or a car."

Judy slit her eyes into a mean frown. "You are so effing weird." She went straight to tell Roy, who liked the excuse to hurt someone, so he waited outside Eddie's English class, and when Eddie walked out, Roy shoved him against the wall and nailed him with five punches to his stomach and ribs. Eddie counted the five and wheezed out a promise that he would have his buddy wreck Roy's house by hitting it with ice at least thirty times for each of those five punches. Roy heard only wheezing, and he laughed. Kids all over the junior high delighted in telling how Roy beat up Eddie the creepy guy, maybe broke some ribs, they said.

"Maybe," one girl declared, "Roy did some permanent damage to his stomach, judging from the way he hunkered over, elbows out from clutching his sides, and walked down the hall sideways like a crab."

Later Eddie asked Dale, "Can you make softball-sized hailstones fall on Roy Jenkins's house?"

"I can," Dale said. "I'll enjoy doing it," and he added that Roy deserved what was coming.

"Yeah," Eddie agreed, "and Judy should never have told Roy to beat me up, so she deserves to have her cat smashed to smithereens."

On Thursday, Eddie and Dale made sure plenty of people saw them during second period. At precisely seventeen minutes after nine, Eddie asked Dale in a loud voice: "What time is it right now?" It was in that precise moment that Clyde Davis, driving too fast on his tractor, ran over a pretty calico cat that he later learned was named Sallie Calley, though in that moment he had no idea he had killed a cat.

But Lucy Ferguson knew. She saw the cat dart into the street, right under the wheel of the tractor. She was making a delivery of yard eggs to the Nelsons, something she did every Thursday at nine fifteen, so when she told her story, she knew exactly what time the cat died, a detail that pleased her to weave into her stories.

Neighbors discussed the events, told of how Lucy waved at Clyde to stop, and he did, and she told him about the cat. Lucy liked to say that he stood over poor Sallie Calley and cried. "He did," Lucy said. "That crusty, rough old rancher actually cried. Over a dead cat." Sometimes Lucy could squeeze out a tear to two as she told the story.

Later, after the junior high kids talked free and loose about how that strange Eddie kid predicted to the minute the cat's death, people of Catclaw discussed whether such a thing was possible. Some said no, and some said yes, though nearly everyone figured Eddie should somehow be held responsible and should be punished, especially since he was so weird.

Eddie said again how great the curry tasted and how wonderful he found the Grandfather Rare Port. He added that he believed the port was stronger than twenty percent and that wine always made him sleepy, so he needed to excuse himself and head home.

After he left, Dale and Robert agreed that damned near anything made Eddie sleepy, and they talked about how it wasn't so much the wine as Eddie's way of using sleep to escape what he called his affliction. "But I understand," Dale said, "because what I can do with water is a curse."

Robert felt inclined to argue, to point out, again, that such gifts, if kept secret, could be put to good use, that it was in the telling, in the hearing, in what people made of the gift that made it feel like a curse, that people wanted his rain and many were willing to injure him to get it. Robert knew Eddie and Dale learned something that first time, the time Eddie told Judy when her cat would die, the time Eddie threatened Roy, then asked Dale to call up a storm.

Dale and Eddie had stood a half a block from Roy's house while Dale located several high, ominous-looking clouds and began weaving his hands and fingers about, all the while holding his face in a tight grimace. Eddie felt the hair prickle on the back of his neck in looking at that determined, hard expression that Dale had as he conjured clouds together and drew them toward Catclaw, pointing them to Roy's house, and the clouds folded in upon each other to roil about in a freezing dance that made hailstones high in the cold air. When they began beating the roof, Dale grinned and cackled like a madman, so Eddie thought this ain't right and told himself to run, though Dale stayed to watch the destruction.

Hailstones destroyed the roof, trimmed branches from a willow by the front door, and broke a hose lying in the yard into green pieces that looked like snakes. The storm stopped as suddenly as it started, and Dale watched the Jenkins family—Roy, his sister, and their parents—come outside where Roy's father burst into tears and his wife offered him comfort though her own cheeks streaked. Even Roy and his sister wept, and Dale whispered "Damn, damn, damn," as he walked home.

The death of Sallie Calley did not please Eddie, and never mind, he told himself, that all he did was predict the cat's death, that he didn't cause it. Later, the kids at school told themselves and any adults who would listen that Eddie killed that cat. Nobody could say how since they knew he was in his second-period class at the time and that it was actually Clyde Davis who ran over the cat with his tractor. But they knew, the kids. They knew. And because of their certainty, Eddie began wondering if he did kill the cat, and he blamed his affliction.

After Dale and Eddie left, Robert sat at the desk staring at the castle moon painting. His two buddies had assumed the clues with the painting referred to places in town. But somehow, he told himself, I know that the answers are not in Catclaw. The ranch, that's where we need to look. The dead starfish, the shark, somehow they were on the Weishuhn ranch, in places he once knew. But Robert had not hiked in the area for what? Forty-two years. Too long to remember many details, he thought, unless in some ways I have selected only a few memories to keep, disposing of others and thus lived one year forty-two times. The other memories could still be there, waiting.

He remembered showing Ophelia his favorite spots, including the cave in the hill above the Texas Colorado River, a day marked forever in his mind. After they stripped for a swim across the river, he took her to the cave's hidden entrance, not high on a hill that dipped into the river where they swam. In the cave they embraced fully for the second time, completely embraced, both wearing only drops of river water, and it was nearly as wonderful as it had been the first time on the sand beside the river.

A slit in the hill hidden behind a huge rock was the entrance to a room, one the Native Americans had used, and so far as Robert could tell, one nobody had found except for him during all the many years since frontier Texans moved the native population elsewhere. He at age seventeen and she at fifteen had consecrated the room, changing each other, changing the feeling he had about the cave, changing the very rocks and the hill that held the cave, even, Robert felt certain, joining in the green voice of all the plant roots under the hill, beyond the hill.

We went back often, he suddenly remembered. And she took to bringing oil paints and a brush. I forgot that, he realized; I covered up other memories with those forty-two years by focusing only on the magic of touching. But of course we didn't make love every minute of our time together: she painted something on the walls of the holy room. Her word *doodled* came to him. Robert couldn't remember what they were, the doodles. I watched her, not what her brush did, he thought, watched the fluid magic of her nude body moving as she hummed, thrust the brush into small bottles of paint, dabbed it on the rock wall.

Was she nude every time she painted in our secret room? Another memory floated into his awareness, a memory of watching that wonderful hand emerging from a sleeve of a jacket to move the brush about on the wall. Then we didn't always swim the river, he whispered to himself, to get to the hill and the cave. Maybe we crossed in a canoe?

When Robert called to ask him to explore a cave on the Weishuhn ranch, Eddie said it was too early to get up, too early to think, but Robert was insistent and talked with excitement Eddie seldom heard in Robert's voice. "My guess," Eddie said, "is that you figured out the meaning of that moon castle painting."

"Not exactly," Robert said. "So you need to come with me and Dale. I'm on the verge of understanding something you can help with." Then Robert astounded Eddie by asking him to bring his strange little inflatable boat and a pump, and Eddie thought hey, he is asking for two favors, maybe three, so now is the time to put the question to him again.

"If I come and bring the boat, I'll expect you will finally tell what you can do."

"Okay, that's fair enough," Robert said.

Dale made a similar remark when Robert called him and urged him to help examine the cave. "It's time," Dale said. "You're in your sixties."

Robert said, "No, I'm fifty nine," and Dale laughed, and Robert promised he would tell. "Today, because it's a good day to have a good day."

"That's weird," Dale said.

"Yes. More weird than you know, yet. Wait until you hear what it is that I can do."

Dale telephoned Eddie who said, "I dread the hearing of it, given how I wrecked my life by telling Marge and the boys about me and death."

Dale understood but said nothing while Eddie told the story again, beginning with his Uncle Craig falling from a stroke, recovering, then calling Eddie, and Eddie drove all the way to San Antonio because Eddie cared more about Craig than anyone else in their family. In San Antonio, Eddie knew before he went into the house, knew even before he parked the car that something would happen inside Craig's brain and he would die in two weeks and one day. Eddie said nothing about such knowledge, not to Craig.

But Eddie said too much to Marge when he got back home feeling so distraught about the impending death. Marge demanded to know when, and Eddie hedged, and Marge pushed, and he blurted out the day, the hour, the minutes. Their teenage boys overheard, and they came downstairs.

"Your dad," Marge said, "knows when people will die, knows the exact date and time and even how."

"Not how," Eddie said, "only some about how, then I guess the rest, and I'll guess that Uncle Craig will have a brain bleed."

"A stroke," Marge said. "So do you know exactly when I will die?" She swept her hand toward their sons. "And them," she demanded, her voice icy and brittle, "do you know when they will die?"

He nodded ever so slightly and the boys looked at each other and ran from the house, and Marge said, "You better not tell me, ever."

The next day she and the boys packed up and left. On their way out, Marge spoke, her words laced with anger: "I can't live with you and your knowing the day and minute I will die." The boys muttered agreement, and they were gone.

"Gone," Eddie told Dale. "Just. Gone."

It was a story Dale had heard before, and as always he said, "We should never talk, you and me, about what we can do."

Dale had a story that was similar in some ways, for Brenda Jane, his wife, left not long after she discovered that Dale was a rainmaker, and even worse, he had that ability but would not use it, refused to cash in on the gift, and before long she also was gone, though she died in a weird car wreck that was somehow not her fault and yet somehow was. Dale felt guilt because he told too much, though Brenda Jane said before she got into the car for her final drive that she had suspected for years.

When Eddie and Dale joined Robert, he was climbing over a barbed wire fence on the Weishuhn ranch. Eddie, handing the inflatable over the fence to Robert, said that he didn't need to know whatever it was that Robert could do. Dale, clutching the tiny pump, said that he agreed with Eddie.

Robert eyed them, brows raised. After they walked to the edge of the river, he said, "You both have learned hard lessons not to talk about your talents, but there has been a shift, a change, a bending in time, so I aim to tell you what I can do, even if it might be better for none of us ever to talk about such matters."

Robert told them.

Eddie hooked the pump to the inflatable, flipped on the switch, and set the 4 A-cell batteries to driving air into the flaccid little boat. As it moved around in the filling, Dale said, "You mean it, I can tell, so I guess it's true that what you can do is listen to plants, but I know plants don't talk, so if you weren't Robert, I just by golly wouldn't believe you and say right to your face you're full of crap."

Eddie recoiled some. "That's a bit harsh," he said to Dale, then turned to Robert. "Listening isn't the same as doing." Eddie made his point with a finger stabbing each word toward Robert.

"That hillside," Robert pointed across the river, "with all its bushes and trees is home for all kinds of interdependent plants, so they are in effect all parts of one large leafy creature. The plants are connected underground, and the roots intertwine and trade food, water, minerals, and the green noise and brown noise they make tells me when the entire collective creature is content and when it is distressed, and this same sprawling creature covers the other hills here, and it's made up of all the roots as well as every branch and leaf and thorn we see above ground."

"Damn," Eddie said.

"Okay then," Dale said.

"The little room in the side of the hill hasn't changed much," Robert said, "maybe not in thousands of years, except when I cleaned it out once after deciding to bring Ophelia here, and I spread that blanket over there that now looks like a layer of dust, but it's still the blanket I put there forty-two years ago."

"Ha!" Eddie said, "a girl."

"You and a girl," Dale said. "That's wonderful, you old dog, you."

"No," Robert said. "Not old. I was young, maybe a dog, but young, and Ophelia a couple of years younger though we were both plenty old to understand what we were doing."

"You dog," Dale said, and Eddie repeated it.

"Okay guys," Robert said. "Enough of that. She also painted." He pointed at the wall.

Eddie chuckled. "She also *painted*? That's funny, you know."

"Okay, okay," Robert said. "We all know what she and I did, so stop talking about it and look at the wall. What are those little doodles?"

Dale, suddenly all business, tapped the wall and said, "If you took a notion to accuse this bit of paint of being a shark, then by golly the fishy-looking thing is a shark."

"Definitely a shark," Eddie said, and the two walked around the room pointing to spots of paint. "There is the strange moon," Dale said, "and that has to be the dead starfish."

"Yeah," Eddie said, "and that might be a raccoon, though I never saw one that long and skinny."

"Alien," Dale said. "An alien raccoon, and lookit these marks, all are larger versions of the ones on the castle moon painting, and check them out from left to right, arranged in the same pattern.”

“There,” Eddie pointed, “the redfish, but no staff and no bit of sky, and hey, there’s some little white streaks over there, lower on the wall, writing, maybe.”

Dale looked around the cave, his palms up in mock puzzlement. “Where,” he asked, “just where could the bed be, the one mentioned in that poem?” He and Eddie looked at the layer of dust that still was a blanket, and they turned grinning to Robert.

“I knew you two would be a huge help,” Robert said, “so thanks to you, I now know where the poem meant for me to look for the staff.” He crossed the room in three steps, reached under the layer of dust that was still a blanket, and pulled out what looked a bit like a deer horn.

“That must be the sibilant staff,” Dale said.

“Maybe,” Eddie said, “except deer horns don’t hiss.”

“This is a talking stick,” Robert said.

“I’ll be jiggered,” Dale said.

Eddie said, “I don’t hear anything.”

Robert could barely contain his excitement. “You hear me talking,” he said, “and if I hand this to you, Dale, here, what happens?”

“Thanks,” Dale said. “I now have permission to talk, now with this talking stick in my hand. I read Indians used to do that with a stick.”

“You both are nuts,” Eddie said.

“Look,” Dale said, “there’s some paper inside the handle.” He pulled the paper out and unrolled it. “Beautiful handwriting, a girl’s. You read it. Aloud.” He handed the paper to Robert.

“That has to be a private love letter,” Eddie said, “so maybe don’t read it aloud?”

“It’s okay,” Robert said, “I no longer have any secrets from you.” He read the letter.

Dale and Eddie listened in solemn silence, and Dale said, “Wow!” in low, reverent tones.

“Yeah, wow,” Eddie said. “But where is Monastir?”

“That’s a beautiful city,” Dale said, “in Tunisia where Ophelia wanted Robert to meet her. Is it possible that she’s still there, waiting?”

“Not likely,” Robert said. “Not after forty-two years, but I sure aim to find out.”

“Those small white lines on the wall,” Eddie said. “We need to look at them.” Robert stepped close to the spot where Eddie pointed.

“It is writing,” Robert said, astounded, and he read aloud, “My father said his family has other houses, one in Amarillo, one in Jasper. Look for me in those if I’m not in Monastir.”

“Over to your right and lower,” Dale said, “more scratches on the wall.”

“Yeah, Eddie said, “I see them, like maybe done with a knife point or a chisel.”

Robert bent low, squinted at the wall. “Words scribbled with something sharp on the very rock.”

“So okay,” Dale said, “read them.”

Robert read: “You waited too long to look for me. The house in Monastir is gone, and the house in Amarillo, both burned, for my gift is a curse. Years slip by like hours.”

“A gift that is a curse,” Dale said. “Can you imagine such a thing?”

“Enough sarcasm,” Robert said. “We don’t know what she means.”

“I think we do,” Eddie said, “because she had two houses burn, so I think she can start fires like Dale can bring rain and like I know the time of deaths and like you can hear plants talk in green and brown.”

"Fire starter," Dale said, "that could fast ruin anybody's life, though if she had me as a friend maybe I could call down water to put out the fires fast enough to keep her family from running away."

"Could be," Eddie said, "and she could scare me into not talking about death to anyone."

"Numbers." Robert tapped the wall. "The note ends with numbers, maybe the date of the scratching, yeah that's it. Ophelia was here ten years ago. She returned and left this note." Robert felt his chest tighten, his heart race and he muttered, "She was here, Ophelia was here in this very cave, and I missed her."

Dale said, "That leaves Jasper. You will look for her in Jasper."

"Yes," Robert said. "It's a small town like Catclaw, so she might like another small town, though it is set in East Texas, in the piney woods, a town almost overwhelmed by the Angelina National Forest. I was there many times when I tried Lamar University down on the coast. Jasper sits in what once was the Big Thicket, with some of it still alive. I went there to hear and talk with the trees, the bushes, as much of the Thicket as I could find."

He found Ophelia's house with bits of the forest on three sides and a scrap of the town on the other. When he rang the doorbell, the young woman who answered, Robert decided instantly, had to be Ophelia's daughter, for she looked exactly like Ophelia did when she was a teenager, so it startled him when she said his name.

"Robert, finally you found me." She opened the door, stepped back, gestured him in. As he shuffled with uncertainty into the house, she said, "I understand your confusion, for I look the same in spite of the years, the decades. You look good, older of course, but younger than I expected."

She explained her gift of being an Evergreen, said it was a curse more than a gift. "If you doubt me," she said, "then certainly I understand."

Robert shook his head. "I'm astounded. You might live and be young for hundreds, maybe thousands of years. That's amazing, and maybe not good for you. There's much to ponder about your evergreeness. But I don't doubt you, for the evidence is you, here, right here, before my eyes. And I know about gifts that are not gifts."

"What do you mean?" Ophelia asked.

"My best friends," he said. "Dale and Eddie are gifted. Dale can summon clouds, make them give up their water as rain or even as hail. Eddie somehow knows when people around him will die. The day, the hour, the minute. He knows that about animals, also. So people fear Dale and Eddie, want to use them, to hurt them. They have lost much because of their gifts, and they work to keep their abilities a secret. Hearing myself talk about Eddie and Dale makes me sound like a madman."

"No. Not now, not here between you and me. After my talk about Evergreens. You are amazing, and I trust you. Tell me more."

"Not much to tell. My buddies have weird powers; but other than that, they are ordinary men."

"I doubt that." Olivia tilted her head, eyed him in an appraising way. "You have some sort of gift. I feel it. You must have a gift your best friends know about. Tell me."

"Plants," he said. "Trees. Even tiny bushes have a way to deal with each other, for mutual benefit, and I hear them speak, though of course they do not speak. Sing, maybe. And I perceive a kind of love among them, though usually it's not obvious."

Ophelia nodded. "No wonder you could tell me all about those trees and bushes that shared the fruit and seeds with us when we were so young, babies really, but old enough to see into each other's souls and learn so much about love in such a short time."

"Yes. No wonder of it. But what would happen if I let it be known that I talk with trees?"

"People would fear you, hunt you down, harm you. They burned my father's homes, two that I watched, others he told me about many years before my birth."

"People." Robert sighed. "Trees are better than most people. Trees love life, can love each other, can speak of love, even act upon it. I have seen evidence right here in the Angelina National Forest. Two trees that became one."

"Oh Robert," she said, "we have so much to tell each other. For now, tell me about those two trees here in my forest."

"By a stream older than the forest," Robert said, "a small stream you no doubt know as Muddy Creek, named by the founders of Jasper, for it runs right through the heart of town. The two trees that became one are lucky enough to still be hidden in the woods west of town."

"How romantic!" she declared, "Two that are one, so lucky even if they are trees, maybe especially if they are trees. Introduce me to them."

"They live close to here, a short drive, then a walk, a wet walk among moist under-growth to the place where the two I'm talking about embraced in a way that set death back for who knows how long."

She clapped her hands, her face lighted with joy. "Take me there. Now."

He showed her, drove to a tiny bridge on a small highway marked 777, parked, and let the green sounds of entangled roots direct him to the larger tree holding the smaller one whose legs, Ophelia noted, had been cut from under it. "So what could the older one do," she said, "but meld the two with sturdy branches to hold it and to share the abundance of roots denied to the smaller tree by a lumberjack's saw. A cruel cut." Ophelia walked around the two that had joined, looked up at the smaller one lifted higher by the growing trunk of the larger one. "This vision brings tears to me," she said, "and even if I do not, cannot believe in signs, there is no way to deny this leafy act. You and I—" she turned to him with sudden intensity, put a hand on his cheek, "you and I might have only decades. I say we take them."

Robert, startled, felt his heart quicken, and said, "I know for a fact that there are no such things as magical signs of any kind to tell people how to live their lives, and yet this tree is a miracle, and I say yes to small decades, to time, to us."

The power lines are down, the great limbs of the venerable old oaks are down, the wreckage is covered in snow and ice.

Andrew Geyer

The boy gasped. "You can't be here," he stammered. "You're missing."
Terry Dalrymple

I liked it that a madman thought me lucid and eloquent.
Jerry Craven

This is a place, both visual and verbal, where both Jules Verne and Isaac Asimov might feel at home. . .

Tom Mack

The Artist, The Writers, the Editor

Jerry Craven

Jerry Craven has lived for extended periods in Southeast Asia, South America, the Middle East, and Europe. His 33 published books include collections of poetry, novels, collections of short stories, and creative nonfiction. The anthologies and journals that have published his short fiction, essays, and poems include *Poetry Australia, Bitterroot International Poetry Quarterly, Liberal and Fine Arts Review, descant, Concho River Review, The Popular Culture Reader, Thema, RiverSedge, Analog*, and *Asimov's*. Three of his plays have been put on stage: two one-act plays and one three-act musical drama (music by A. William Hinson). He is founding editor and director of Lamar University Literary Press and founding editor (along with Robert Whitsitt) of the international literary journal *Amarillo Bay*. His professional memberships include The Texas Institute of Letters and the Science Fiction & Fantasy Writers of America.

Terry Dalrymple

Founder of *Concho River Review* and member of the
Texas Institute of Letters, Terry Dalrymple has
published numerous short fictions, essays, and articles
in a variety of journals,magazines, and anthologies. In
addition to having edited one literary journal and
guest-editing another, he has edited *Texas Soundtrack*,
a collection of stories inspired by Texas music, and has
co-edited *Texas Weather*, a collection of poetry, fiction,
and nonfiction, with Laurence Musgrove. His published
books of fiction include *Dancing on Barbed Wire*
(co-written with Andrew Geyer and Jerry Craven),
Love Stories (Sort Of), *Salvation*, and *Fishing for
Trouble*. He was recently named Distinguished English
Professor Emeritus by Angelo State University in San
Angelo, Texas, where he spends his time writing, taking
photographs, and gardening.

Andrew Geyer

Andrew Geyer's ninth book, the story cycle *Lesser Mountains* (Lamar University Press, 2019), won a 2020 Independent Publisher Book Award (IPPY) for U.S. South - Best Regional Fiction. His other individually authored books are *Dixie Fish*, a novel; *Siren Songs from the Heart of Austin*, a story cycle; *Meeting the Dead*, a novel; and *Whispers in Dust and Bone*, a story cycle that won the silver medal for short fiction in the *Foreword Magazine* Book of the Year Awards and a Spur Award for short fiction from the Western Writers of America. He is the co-author, with Jerry Craven and Terry Dalrymple, of the hybrid story cycle *Dancing on Barbed Wire*. Geyer also co-authored *Parallel Hours*, an alternative history/sci fi novel; and *Texas 5X5*, another hybrid story cycle from which one of his stories won a second Spur Award for short fiction. He co-edited the composite anthology *A Shared Voice* with Tom Mack. A member of the Texas Institute of Letters and the South Carolina Academy of Authors, Geyer currently serves as English Department Chair at the University of South Carolina Aiken and Fiction Editor for *Concho River Review*.

Tom Mack

Dr. Tom Mack holds the rank of USC Distinguished Professor Emeritus. During his thirty-nine years on the faculty of the University of South Carolina Aiken, 25 of those years as chair of the English Department, he was frequently recognized for his teaching, scholarship, and public service. In 2008, the USC Board of Trustees awarded him the prestigious Carolina Trustee Professorship; and in 2014, he received the Governor's Award in the Humanities. Dr. Mack remains active in retirement. He is the author/editor of eight books. He also continues to write his "Arts and Humanities" column, appearing each weekend since 1990 in *The Aiken Standard*. For his museum and gallery reviews in the weekly *Post and Courier/Free-Times* (Columbia, SC), he was honored by the South Carolina Press Association.

Besides serving as the current chair of the board of South Carolina Humanities, the state's affiliate of the National Endowment for the Humanities, Mack was elected a Lifetime Member of the board of governors of the South Carolina Academy of Authors, which manages the state's literary hall of fame.